LOST GIRL

Hidden Book One

COLLEEN VANDERLINDEN

Lost Girl: Hidden Book One
Colleen Vanderlinden

Published in the United States
by Building Block Studios LLC

ISBN 0615931855
ISBN-13 978-0615931852

http://www.colleenvanderlinden.com/lostgirl
http://www.buildingblockstudios.com

DEDICATION

For Roger

Best friend, love of my life.
Thanks for all the times
you said "you should do that."

I finally did!

CONTENTS

ACKNOWLEDGMENTS

This book would not have happened without the support of my amazing family. Thanks and hugs and kisses to my awesome children for their support, patience, and understanding that sometimes, I am not all quite here.

Thanks to Hidden's earliest readers for their never-ending encouragement and enthusiasm for Molly's story. Without that, I don't know how much I would have actually written. Many hugs to Jayna Longstreet, Kellie Roach, Kathy Kloba, Michelle Kay. You ladies rock.

And, finally, thanks to my husband, who does all of the technical stuff and designed my book cover and never once looked at me funny when I said I was writing about demons. I love you.

CHAPTER ONE

I shouldered my messenger bag as I walked out of the library and out onto campus. I could feel a migraine forming behind my eyes, and the sweltering, humid weather was not helping. I looked at the students lounging in the courtyard, talking on phones or goofing off with friends, as I walked to the parking structure. Lucky brats.

I couldn't help feeling more than a twinge of irritation as I caught their thoughts. This one worried about his girlfriend, a girl deeply contemplated the pros and cons of a nose job, and another moped about how much she hated working.

Join the club, kid, I thought, rolling my eyes. I wasn't much older than most of the underclassmen I passed, but I felt as if I'd lived whole lives longer than they had.

I stopped, as always, near the bulletin board just before I crossed Anthony Wayne Drive to the parking structures. Scanned it. A mix of job postings, recruitment notices, lost dog/car keys/book notices. Two fliers of missing girls. The first I'd already seen. I'd be taking care of that later that night. The second was new to me.

Marja Szymanski, 19, of Hamtramck. I pulled out my phone and took a picture of the flier. I would have liked something a little more detailed, but I'd research it when I had a minute. I shook my head. Impossible to keep up with them all.

When I got to the parking structure, I waved to the attendant, who waved at me with a hearty "hey, Molly!" just like he did every day, and climbed the four flights to where I was parked. By the time I got to my car, I was sweating as if I'd run a marathon.

I looked at my car, a pitch-black 1970 Barracuda I'd bought off of a little old man at a steal after I'd found his granddaughter and brought her home safe. I ran my hands along the trunk lovingly. I knew it was ridiculous. It was a car. A method of transportation. But it was mine, and it was bad ass.

I got in, rolled the window down, and turned up the stereo. AC/DC blared. Screw the migraine.

I sped out of the parking structure and headed toward Cass, then snaked toward Gratiot and toward home. I noticed people giving me weird, worried looks. Easy to catch their thoughts: young chick, in an expensive car, with the windows down, in this neighborhood? I smirked. I was the scariest thing out here.

I drove through the east side, finally reaching my neighborhood. "Neighborhood" was being generous. The houses on the blocks immediately surrounding mine, as well as on my block, had been leveled years ago. I lived on a vast urban prairie. Tall grass and ghetto palm as far as the eyes could see, except for the six lots I'd claimed as my own over the years. Mine. I pulled the car up into the garage, parked, and got out. I shut the garage doors behind me, and my two German shepherds loped up to me, tongues lolling, tails wagging. Kurt and Courtney. I was a 90s brat, after all.

I scratched them both behind the ears, patted them on their sides, and headed up the back steps to the kitchen door. When I got inside, I took a deep breath. Home. Finally.

I made a salad and grabbed some iced tea, sat at my 50s Formica table and ate it, listening to the Tigers on the radio. The quiet calm that surrounded my house was like an ointment that soothed away the irritations of my day job, the stresses of my night job. Hopefully, I wouldn't need the day job much longer. I'd paid cash for the house and car. I just wanted to build up a nest egg so I could afford basic expenses for a while, and then I would quit. And have time for more important things. I spent the next few hours napping and doing research for that evening's jobs.

At around ten, I started suiting up. Black top, long sleeves. Black cargo pants. Black Chucks. I brushed my long nearly-black hair mechanically, almost in a trance as I plotted that night's business. I put a variety of things into my pockets. Zip ties, tear gas, a pearl-handled switchblade. A prepaid cell phone. I sighed and looked at the mirror on my dresser. Not at my reflection; I knew what I'd see there; lots of pale skin and dark circles. But at the photograph taped to the upper left-hand corner. Forced myself to really look. The reason I did what I did, the shame I wouldn't let myself forget.

"Time to go save some lost girls," I murmured to the photograph. Then I patted it, gently, four times with my fingertips. Four taps, four lost girls who needed to be found. And that's what I would do.

I drove down Gratiot, to a neighborhood that looked a lot like mine, but, impossibly enough, even deader. Desolate.

I parked a few blocks away from where I needed to be, pulling into a garage that was leaning precariously, its wooden clapboards rotting, showing just a few remaining stubborn specks of white paint. Then I got out, stood at the window and lifted the pocket binoculars to my eyes, watched the corner on the next block. I'd picked up this location snooping around where one of the suspects in the kidnapping hung out. He wouldn't be alone. And the girls were alive, and relatively alright, so far. Of course, I'd known they'd still be alive. There was money to be made.

I could hear the squeak of a storm door's hinges creaking as the wind blew. A Detroit version of an Old West ghost town.

I watched a dark blue van pull up to the corner and three men got out. Early, eager for a payday. My cue.

I stalked out of the garage, not rushing, but purposeful. The three men were tense, watching in the opposite direction. Not talking. Feet shuffling, arms crossed over their chests.

"Hey, assholes," I said, my voice cutting the silence of the night. I could feel my power coursing through me, welcomed it. My invisible armor, my weapon.

There was a lot of fumbling, some swearing, and when I reached them, I had three guns pointed at my face.

It wasn't anything personal, of course. I would be pissed, too, if someone interrupted a nice paying deal like this one.

They stood there, guns pointed, breath ragged. Nervous, angry. In the distance, I could hear the typical night noises: cars, sirens, the occasional pop-pop-pop of someone shooting a gun. Hopefully into the air.

I sighed. "You hate guns," I said, feeling the power roll off of my body toward the men. "You are afraid of guns. More than anything, you want to put the guns down." Glazed looks in their eyes, then they did just that, looks of disgust contorting their features as they dropped the guns, as if they'd been holding steaming piles of shit instead of metal. "Now. Hand over the girls." Power still emanating from my voice.

"No fuckin' way," the largest of the men said, shaking off my power and aiming a punch at my face. I ducked it easily, kicked out and heard a satisfying squish as my heel came into contact with his groin. He fell down, whimpering. His comrades were on me. The short one was more vicious, reaching for a knife tucked into his waistband. But he was overconfident. He came too close, and I kicked out hard at the side of his knee. Heard a crack, then a scream, and he fell. I kicked his knife into the tall grass nearby.

"Okay. Your turn," I said, moving closer to the third man, who had backed away. He took one look at his buddies writhing on the concrete, put his hands into the air, and shook his head.

"This was their deal, lady. They just brought me along for back up," he said, a bright sheen of sweat across his forehead. "I don't want any trouble from you."

"You pussy," the little one shouted from his spot on the ground. I kicked him in the stomach and he went back to whimpering.

"Are you going to hand over the girls, then?" I asked, as if we hadn't been interrupted at all. I wished they could hurry this along. It was hot, and I hated every abandoned neighborhood that wasn't *my* abandoned neighborhood. They gave me the creeps, no matter how much time I spent in them. Their loneliness, the sense of desolation and desperation, of being forgotten, was overwhelming. It was almost a physical thing, and it weighed on me.

He nodded, walked over to the van, and opened the back doors. The little guy started yelling at him again, and I kicked him in the ribs.

"Shut the hell up," I muttered, power lacing my words.

The guy led three teenage girls out of the back of the van, wrists tied behind their backs, duct tape over their mouths. Two black girls, one Latina. Pretty, thin girls who would have made someone lots of money. I felt relief mingled with disgust. It took everything in my power not to kill the two men whimpering on the ground. As it was, I gave them each a well-aimed kick to the groin, as much for the girls' benefit as my own. I gestured for the girls to come toward me, and they did, slowly, dazed, as if they weren't sure this was for real.

I looked at the guy who had let them go. "You did the

right thing tonight," I said, pushing as much power as I could into my voice. "You want to stay out of this business. You want to get a job, go back to school. Stay away from these assholes," I said, giving the loudmouth one another kick. "If I hear about you involved in anything like this again, I will find you." I paused, felt the fear rolling off of him. "And you really don't want that to happen."

"Yes, ma'am," he said. He got into the van and drove off after one more glance at me. Didn't even look at the guys on the ground. Loyalty.

I looked at the two remaining thugs. "And you two," I said, filling my voice, my eyes, with power. I watched their eyes glaze over. "You two are going to stay right the fuck where you are until morning. Once the sun comes up, you can move again. And when you do get up, you are going to the nearest Detroit police precinct, and you're going to turn yourselves in for the abduction of Amber Johnson, Shanti Williams, and Maria Alvarez. And you are going to tell the police who you were going to sell them to. It will be done," I finished, and power thrummed in the air around me.

They both nodded.

I shook my head and turned to the girls, who were looking at me in shock. I walked over to them and tried, as gently as possible, to remove the duct tape from their mouths, then I cut the ties confining their hands. I could sense intense fear, disbelief, and a glimmer of hope coming off of them.

"Are you alright?" I asked softly.

They all nodded. "Thank you so much. Thank you," the petite one, Shanti, started saying. She made the sign of the cross with her hand and bowed her head. Praying.

"I have a car nearby. I can drive you home." By now, all three were crying in relief. I started walking down the block, where I'd parked earlier. The three girls followed, hands clasped as if they were afraid to let go of each other.

I could hear their soft sobs. I kept my eyes peeled for any trouble. Relief when we got back to the car without any incident. I opened the doors and looked back at the two would-be salesmen. They were still laying right where I'd left them. I could have ordered them to go to the precinct right away, but I wanted them to suffer. Pissing themselves and getting bitten by mosquitoes was nothing compared to what I wanted to do to them.

I climbed into the driver's seat and slammed my door. Maria and Amber were in the back, and Shanti rode shotgun. I started the car, and AC/DC blared from the speakers. I turned it down with a grimace. "Sorry," I said, tossing a smile at Shanti.

"This music suits you, I think," Shanti said, turning the radio back up. "Back in Black" echoed through the night.

As we drove toward the Southwest side, where the girls had been taken on their way home from softball practice, I caught Shanti peeking at me every once in a while. Maria and Amber were doing the same thing from the back seat. Their thoughts were a jumble of being thankful they were going home and wondering who the hell the crazy lady was. All three, in the past five minutes, had told themselves they had to take self-defense classes. I just drove on.

I wasn't much for conversation. Besides, I had a couple of other things on my mind. Currently, it was the asshole in the black pickup who had been following us since we'd left the neighborhood where I'd found the girls. I kept an eye on him in the rearview. He didn't seem to be trying to catch me, but he was definitely tailing the car. I circled aimlessly through a few neighborhoods, just to make sure. He stayed with us. I sighed. Great. One more thing to deal with. Looked at my watch. I was behind schedule already.

"How did you do that?" Shanti finally asked.

"I knew a few things from self-defense classes," I said, shrugging, hoping it would be enough. But I knew better. Shanti shook her head.

"No, I mean *all* of that. How did you know where we were? How did you beat the crap out of those two guys? How did you just convince them to let us go? Are you FBI or something?"

I was silent for a minute. "Let's go with 'something.'" I saw Shanti shake her head, and I threw a small smile in the girl's direction.

We reached the Southwest side, streets flanked with old brick bungalows. Virgin Mary statues dotted front lawns, and somewhere in the night, I could hear bass thumping and a dog barking. I dropped Amber off first, then Maria, and the amazed squeals that greeted each girl's appearance went right to my heart.

When I pulled up to the curb in front of Shanti's house, the girl hesitated. We both looked up at the house. Every window was lit. A candle burned on the front porch.

"Thank you," Shanti finally said. "You're the one who's been finding the lost girls, aren't you?" I was silent. Shanti watched me, and smiled. "I don't know how you did that, but thank you."

"You're welcome. Go on, now," I said softly. "You've got people waiting for you."

The girl nodded, then leaned over, and, to my surprise, folded me in a big, strong hug that nearly took my breath away. "Thank you so much," she whispered again.

I hugged her back. Our eyes met for just a second, then Shanti bounded out of the car with a smile. As soon as she stepped on the bottom porch step, screams erupted from the house, and about a dozen people came running out. I smiled to myself and pulled away.

Of course, now I had to deal with the asshole in the pickup truck.

He was still there, not even a car length behind me. He wanted me to notice him. It was obvious the driver didn't want the girls. I figured he had a score to settle with me. It wasn't as if I didn't have any enemies.

I drove through downtown on my way toward my next

stop, and the truck tailed me the whole way. Finally, I pulled up to a curb near Campus Martius, slammed the 'Cuda into park, and got out of the car. The truck pulled up behind me and the driver turned off the engine.

I leaned against my door, arms crossed over my chest, glaring at the truck. A few cars drove by. I could hear the noise from whatever concert was going on over at Comerica Park in the distance.

Finally, the driver's side door opened, and a mountain emerged from the truck. At least, "mountain" was the best way I could describe the man that stepped out and slammed the door. He was tall, easily 6'6 or so. Broad. Dark brown hair, cut short. Strong chin, covered with dark stubble. Piercing blue eyes that, with just one glance, made me feel as if he saw much more than he should. He walked toward me with a very "don't fuck with me" attitude, one I could appreciate from my own method. He reached me, and stood still in front of me. We just watched each other, like two wolves sizing each other up. I knew it was immature, but I refused to say the first word. He was following me, he could damn well talk first. I hated people who didn't mind their own business.

And this guy was even more disturbing. I could feel power freaking rolling off of him. Power to rival my own. Dangerous.

He seemed just as stubborn as I was, but more patient. He just stood there, arms crossed like mine, watching me. Silence, the sizing up between the two of us dragged on for several slow minutes as life went on around us.

I let out an irritated sigh. "Okay, fine. What do you want?" I finally said.

"That was some work you did back there," he said, his voice a low rumble, two stones grating against one another. It sent a shiver up my spine, and I tried to ignore it.

"Who are you?"

"Mind control is a very dangerous skill, Molly," he said,

as if he hadn't heard my question.

Fuck. "You never saw me," I said, pushing power into my voice.

He shook his head. "That doesn't work on me. You'll have to try something else."

"Who. Are. You?" I asked again, standing up straight. My hands flexed into fists. Habit.

"You going to beat me up? I'm not some street thug," he said.

"Am I going to have to?"

"The last thing I want to do is get into a fight with you."

"You can start by telling me your name then, and why you were following me," I said, lowering my hand and grasping the canister of tear gas in my pocket.

"You're not going to need that. My name is Nain."

I looked up at him, narrowing my eyes. "Is that your real name?"

"Close enough. *Le Nain Rouge*, Red Dwarf, Red Gnome, Lutin. I prefer Nain."

"Right. Oookay. I don't believe in fairy tales."

"It's not any more far-fetched than someone controlling people with her mind," he said, meeting my eyes. Pretty eyes, a deep sapphire, practically glowing under the street lights.

"You don't look particularly red, or, you know, gnome-like, to me," I said.

"That's one of my forms. I don't do that anymore." Anger, regret.

"Right," I said again. Dude was a complete nutcase. "You cause trouble. Harbinger of doom, all that shit."

"People always get that fucked up. Where does it say that the harbinger of doom is the one that actually caused the doom? Maybe the so-called harbinger is there because he saw it coming and is trying to stop the doom."

"Uh-huh. So you're saying you had nothing to do with the '67 riots?"

"Trying to stop the fighting."

"Or with burning the city to the ground in 1805?"

"Chasing the guy who actually did it."

"And you didn't, in fact, curse Cadillac?"

"That, I did. And he had it coming," he said. Snarled, to be more accurate.

"Right. So you're claiming to be over three hundred years old, and you can change into a little red dwarf. And I'm supposed to believe that you're not completely insane?" I hissed, feeling my power spike in response to my emotions.

He just watched me. He was so serious looking I almost wanted to believe him. Almost.

"Okay. I don't know how you found me, or what you think I can do. You stay away from me or you're going to be wearing your balls as earrings. Do you understand?" I started getting into my car.

Crazy people, I thought as I slammed the door behind me. He was still standing there, next to the car.

Or we can just converse telepathically, he thought at me.

I got out of the car again, looked up at him. "Shit."

He gave a short bark of a laugh, crossed his arms over his chest.

You can really read my thoughts?

Yes, I really can.

How did you find me? I could feel a headache coming on, always a side effect of reading thoughts, never mind actually conversing telepathically.

"We can just talk," he said, seeming to understand my discomfort. "Once you've had more practice with it, it will hurt less."

"You're a telepath, too, then?" I asked, annoyed with myself for continuing to talk with this crazy person.

He nodded. "In some ways, I'm a lot like you. I can read thoughts. I can communicate telepathically with someone who has the same skill, though it's been awhile since I've come across another."

"Are there many?"

He shrugged. "It's always safe to assume that there are others around. Most don't quite realize what it is that they can do." He stopped talking, met my eyes again. "It would be a good idea to learn to shield your thoughts. You are wide open, Molly. That can be dangerous."

I looked at him. Concentrated. "I can't pick yours up."

"I have a lot of practice shielding. It's automatic at this point."

"So someone can only hear your thoughts if you want them to?" I asked, interest piqued.

Yes. And then, only that person. No one else.

I thought about that. Any telepath around could hear everything I thought. Dangerous, for sure, if any of them were like me. I looked around, watching the shadows, as always.

"But, there is at least one big difference between you and me," he said, as if he'd never stopped talking. "I can't control thoughts. I can't put my thoughts in other people's heads, make them act on my command. That's a whole different level of power."

"And you want something from me, is that it?' I asked.

"No. All I want is to help you learn to control your telepathy. Learn to shield yourself."

"There's no such thing as something for nothing," I murmured, mostly to myself.

He was quiet for a bit. I was starting to think he hadn't heard me. "You're right. I do want something," he finally said. I felt my stomach twist. My power was reacting weirdly around him, and it was only helping to throw me off even more.

"What?"

"I want you to come and work for me."

"I work alone," I said.

"Just come, meet with me and some of my associates," he said.

"I work alone," I said again, slowly and deliberately, stopping and looking him dead in the eyes. "I am not a team player. I don't even like most people. I'm not interested."

I felt irritation rolling off of him in waves. The first time he'd lost his cool at all, I realized. Most people lost their patience with me much quicker than that.

"Holy shit," he said, staring at me.

"What?" I asked, my stomach turning in response to the spike of surprise I'd picked up from him.

"What was that?" he asked. "You can sense emotions?"

"Stay the fuck out of my mind," I said, stomping my foot.

"Then learn to shield yourself," he shot back.

"It's a real violation, that you keep doing that," I said to him, irritated and stalking back to the car. "Just because you can, doesn't mean you should."

I felt a tiny bit of guilt coming from him. But then he said, "Yes, and putting thoughts in someone's mind, making them do what you want, isn't a violation at all."

I spun on him, glared up into his face. "You know what? Screw you. I do that, and I save lives. You followed me tonight. Those three girls would have been out on a corner in a week. I saved them from that." I stopped, seething. I pointed at him. "And if it requires putting a fear of guns, a hatred of crime, and a terror of ever meeting me in a dark alley into any of these assholes, that's what I'll do."

"Easy to abuse that power," he said mildly, "once you decide you've got something to prove."

"I don't have anything to prove. I have a skill, and I use it. Stay away from me," I said again, getting into the car. I slammed the door behind me, cranked up the stereo, and took off, tires screeching for good effect, into the night.

I looked at my watch. Fuck. I was way behind. I better not have failed my other lost girl, or he was going to pay. I sped toward the east side again. Checked the gas gauge. I really should get a more fuel-efficient car. Gas prices were killing me.

CHAPTER TWO

I turned onto a mostly empty street, not too far from the Grosse Pointe Park border. So close to that moneyed life, yet worlds away. It had been a nice neighborhood once upon a time. People were trying to rejuvenate it, evidenced by the three large renovated houses that stood near Jefferson. The rest of the street was desolate, dark. I parked the car and got out.

I stood and just listened, watched. It was so quiet, which made my job easier. Noisy places were a pain in the ass. Easy to get surprised when there were a lot of background noises, crowds of people. I often thought how stupid my particular brand of criminals were. They hid people in emptiness. They didn't realize that the best place to hide something was in plain sight.

I could hear something further down the block. Thumping, other muffled noises. I started walking toward the sounds. Slowed, focused, followed the sound of what I now knew was a woman; my lost girl. I reached out with my thoughts, caught them : "Oh my god I'm going to die. He's going to kill me. Please God watch over Jakey for me." More thumping. The woman was kicking the sides of her prison. A trunk? My telepathy was useful, but it wasn't perfect. If the person wasn't thinking clearly, and anyone as terrified as this woman wasn't, then it made mind-reading a lot trickier. I was just relieved I could hear the woman's thoughts at all. It meant I wasn't too late.

I kept walking. One hand around my pepper spray. Another around my knife. I kept following the noises, the sound of pounding and kicking, toward a house. I crept toward it, listening. The noise was coming from the garage. The house was clearly abandoned; the garage barely standing. I gingerly pulled the garage door open. There was a red Taurus parked inside. The pounding noise was coming from inside the trunk. Bingo.

The noise in the trunk ceased, and I heard a whimper. A name came from the woman, along with an overwhelming wave of fear. Brandon.

"I'm not Brandon," I said. The woman stayed quiet, but I felt surprise, hope from her. "I'm going to get you out of there, Teresa. Okay?"

Teresa started sobbing, and I felt relief from her. *Police*, the woman thought.

There wasn't any point in correcting her. If believing I was the police made her feel better, she could go on thinking it. Fewer questions that way.

I looked around and found a crowbar on the floor in one corner of the garage. It was rusty, covered in spider webs, but it would work. I worked it inside the trunk, near the lock, and pushed with all my might. Harder. "Just hold on," I said to Teresa again. I put all my weight on it, and could feel the lock starting to give.

I was still working at it when I heard gravel crunch behind me, a motor. A car door slammed, as did a whole bunch of panicked, angry thoughts. Lovely. Ex-hubby dearest had arrived. I cursed under my breath as I heard him running up the driveway.

"What the hell is going on here?" a man shouted, heading toward me. Teresa gave a cry from inside the trunk.

"Brandon?" I asked, freeing the crowbar and holding it nonchalantly at my side. My pepper spray was back in my hand.

"You shouldn't be here," he said. "Just, put it down." I hefted the crowbar, glared at him. *I have to kill this bitch. No other way, bury her and Teresa together and I'm done.* "You really think a crow bar is going to do anything against me?" he said aloud. He laughed. I could feel anger, anxiety rolling off of him. It practically had an odor, it was so strong.

"If you're so sure, come on and get me," I snapped.

He pointed the gun at me. "Put it down."

"Oh, fuck you."

He let off a shot, then another. One grazed my thigh, but I bit back a yelp and tried to ignore it. The amount of fear and anger flowing around me was practically making me dizzy. I started walking toward him, and pushed out with my power. "You're going to toss the gun down, now, Brandon," I said, my voice full of power. He hesitated. "Now," I commanded, and the garage creaked around us. He put the gun down, and the fear coming from him was absolute. I felt strengthened by it, almost giddy. "Step back," I said. He did, and I kicked the gun behind me, under the car. I could feel blood dripping down my leg from where I'd been shot. I walked over to him, and he shook off enough of my influence to react. He got a hold of the ends of my hair, and yanked. I sprayed the pepper spray, then punched him in the face, hard. A wet sound, and then he dropped to the ground, whimpering.

"Yeah, big, tough man, kidnapping your ex," I muttered. "You know, it's pieces of shit like you that make it so I can never take a fucking vacation." He started to stand up, but not quickly enough. I used the crowbar to knock him out, then bound his hands and feet with zip ties, and put some duct tape over his mouth. "Every damn day, I'm out here chasing one of you assholes down, you know that? Every. Damn. Day." Once he was secure, I went back to the car and jammed the crowbar into the

17

trunk, forcing it open.

The woman inside, Teresa, was tiny and scared to death, hands and feet bound with duct tape. A scarf or something was tied around her mouth. She was crying, and I started working at the gag so she could talk. She had been in there for a few days. The odor was awful. I wanted to hit Brandon a few more times. Forced back a snarl.

"Calm down," I ordered, gently, just a little power in my voice.

"It's you. The Angel," the woman finally said, still crying.

I grimaced. Of all the monikers the media could have given me... "Do you need a doctor?" I asked.

The woman shook her head. She looked toward Brandon. "Is he dead?" she whispered.

"No. Just unconscious. For now."

"I wish he was," the woman said, staring at him. I was tempted to hand her the crowbar.

"I'm sure. I'm about to call the police to come pick him up. Do you have a way to get out of here?"

"That's my car," she said, pointing at the Taurus. "Brandon took the keys when he grabbed me."

I went over to the unconscious man and dug through his pockets, coming up with some condoms, a pack of cigarettes, and the car keys. I tossed them to Teresa, then rolled Brandon out of the way.

Teresa watched me. "I'll go to the police about him. I'll tell them where he is, and what happened," she said.

"They might not believe you," I said. "They might think you did this," I gestured at Brandon.

"Nah. I have the rope burns and bruises to prove it. And everyone knows you find lost girls," she said, smiling. "Thank you so much," she said, and started crying again.

I just nodded. Uncomfortable. "Okay. You should get going," I said. Teresa nodded, then climbed into the car. I watched her drive into the night, gave the unconscious Brandon a kick for good measure, then headed down the street. Exhaustion had officially set in, and I had to work in the morning.

I walked back to my car, stumbling a little. I could feel my leg burning where I'd been shot. It wasn't bleeding as much anymore, though. I got in and tore through the streets toward home.

When I got there, I scratched Kurt and Courtney behind the ears, then headed into the house. I went to my office first, faced the two large bulletin boards on the wall. Moved the photos of Shanti, Amber, Maria, and Teresa from the "lost" board to the "found." I placed the pushpins precisely into the corners of each photo, ran my fingertips over each one. I inspected the wall again. The "lost" board was full. The "found" board was filling up. And the third board, the one for girls I'd been too late for... that one had more pictures on it than it should have. I looked at their faces, the ones I'd been too slow to save, thought their names like a litany.

I looked back to the "lost" board. Shook my head. Feeling helpless now wouldn't help them.

I limped down to the kitchen to get something to eat. I made a peanut butter sandwich and took it into the living room, flicked on a lamp and the television.

The local station interrupted Letterman with a news flash. A female reporter stood in front of one of the houses I had dropped the girls off at earlier in the night. It felt like so long ago.

A voice over said. "We interrupt this broadcast for a breaking news bulletin. Four people who went missing earlier this week have been miraculously returned to their families, from all reports, by the Angel. We're on the scene with one of these people now." I watched and shook my head. Media was getting stupid about this now.

"I'm here on the Southwest side with the family of Shanti Williams, who, as you may remember, along with her friends Maria Alvarez and Amber Bryant, went missing earlier this week. Witnesses said they saw three men push them into a van and drive away. Tonight, all three girls are back with their families, safe and sound, and, from all reports, they have the Angel to thank! Shanti, can you tell me what happened?"

"The guys had us in an empty neighborhood. They were about to sell us to someone. We were in the van, tied up, and they were outside. And all of a sudden, we heard yelling and sounds like punching or kicking, and we were scared to death, thinking how much worse can this get, you know?"

"And then the van doors opened, and there she was. The woman who's been finding lost girls," Shanti said, and smiled through her tears. "She beat the hell out of two much bigger men, managed to get their guns away from them, got us out of there and drove us home. I've never seen anything like that my whole life. Those who don't believe Jesus answers prayers, you're wrong. I prayed for help, and He sent her. I know it." And then the tears started falling.

The camera cut back to the studio. "We're also getting reports that Teresa Marson, missing from her home for over a week, has also been found and returned to her family."

The camera cut to another neighborhood. "I'm here in East English Village, where Teresa Marson returned home about a half hour ago." A crowd outside the home erupted in cheers. "Teresa, can you tell us how you made it home?"

Teresa appeared on screen. Face bruised, but looking happy. "My ex-husband, Brad, kidnapped me because I wouldn't go back to him. He bought a gun yesterday," she said, and her voice started to tremble. "He knew people were looking for me. He was going to get rid of me tonight, he told me."

"And I was laying in the trunk, waiting to die, and I heard someone working at the trunk, like they were trying to pry it open. But then I heard a fight start. Brad had come back, and he wasn't happy to find her there."

"Her?"

"The woman who rescued me. The one who finds lost girls. She fought Brad off, knocked him out, tied him up. Then she got me out of the car. I hope she's okay," she said, her forehead creasing. "Brad shot her, but she wouldn't let me take her to the hospital," she said, and then she started crying.

I clicked the television off and sat in the living room in silence. It had always been my intention to keep a low profile. I didn't want the media circus. Being known made it so much harder to fly under the radar, which was necessary for the way I did things. I'd been toying with the idea of taking memories of me away from those I saved. Too many people now knew what I looked like, what I drove. It was only going to complicate matters. I'd been against the idea of stealing their memories, because it seemed wrong. But there was no other way to work this. I sighed and closed my eyes.

I had just dozed off when I heard the dogs snarling, and the doorbell rang. "What now?" I growled into the empty room, and headed toward the door. I looked out the small window and groaned.

"Are you kidding? What are you doing here?" I muttered as I opened the front door.

CHAPTER THREE

"You got shot. I'm here to check on you." The asshole from the truck. Nain. I glared at him.

"Were you following me again?" I was on the verge of shouting.

"I wasn't following you. I went home. It was on the news," he said, his voice low and annoyingly reasonable. "If you don't let me in I'm going to call an ambulance."

"Don't," I warned.

"Then let me in," he said.

"You are a pain in the ass," I said, unlocking the storm door and pushing it open. He followed me inside and closed the door. We walked through the living room, into the kitchen. I reached the kitchen sink and turned around, crossed my arms, looked at him.

"Let me see," he said. I swore the floor vibrated with his voice.

I pointed at my leg. My jeans were soaked in blood, and a hole was on my upper thigh. Another pair of pants, ruined.

"That doesn't help. Let me actually see it," he said, irritation lacing his voice.

I sighed. "You don't need to. It's already closed up."

He met my eyes, and I felt a spike of surprise. "You're telling me you can heal yourself?"

I looked down, avoiding his eyes. He saw too much. "I can juggle, too. Best circus freak, ever." Then I looked up at him, waiting for him to leave. He just stood there, watching me.

I started cleaning up from making my sandwich, just to have something to do.

"Four women. Not a bad night's work," Nain said, leaning against the wall.

I shrugged. "It's not enough."

"To those four families, it's everything."

"And to all those girls out there who are still lost, it's nothing," I said.

I wondered when he would leave, already. He didn't seem to be in any hurry. I sighed and walked over to the fridge, grabbed a pitcher and a plate of fruit. I put it all on the table, then grabbed two glasses and set them down as well.

"You're here. Might as well take a load off," I said, sitting down in one of the vinyl-covered chairs.

He did. "Thanks." We sat in silence for a bit, sipping iced tea. "I can tell that you want to Hulk-smash me."

I sighed. "Yeah. I like my privacy. For obvious reasons. I keep contact with people to a minimum. It's exhausting to be around others too much, all these thoughts coming at me, feelings surrounding me, and I can't get away." I grabbed a strawberry, bit into it. I noticed Nain watching me, and felt something like dread in the pit of my stomach.

"If you learned to shield yourself…"

I waved his comment away. "I know. I know. You want me to join your team. What are you, like the Avengers or something?"

He smiled. It did nothing to comfort me, a show of white teeth, a snarl as much as anything else. "Maybe. I find people like you, like me, who can do things. People who are already trying to use their abilities for good. And

23

we pool our resources and work together. Some of them don't function well in society, some have nowhere to go, so they live downtown in a loft, with me."

"Superhero complex. And I'm the one with something to prove," I muttered.

"I don't have a superhero complex. Look, if you're good with people, you go into teaching, or nursing, or something. If you're good with math, you go into engineering or whatever, right? We're good at other things. Why not use it?"

"I'm already using it," I reminded him. "And despite what you seem to think, I'm not in any danger of misusing it." I leaned forward, resting my elbows on the table, and looked at him. "What are you?"

I sensed discomfort from him. "What do you mean?"

"You're not human." I didn't know how I knew it. He looked completely human. He was something different. And I was confused by the way my power responded to him, almost as if it recognized and welcomed his power. It irritated me. A lot.

"You already knew that," he reminded me.

"Right. So, what are you, really?"

He just stared at me. I met his eyes, held. He shook his head.

"Well?" I asked.

"Demon," he said, voice quiet. Chills went up my spine.

"A demon." I looked at the ceiling, took a deep breath. "If you are a demon, shouldn't you be trying to kill me?" I wondered how fast I could reach the butcher knife on the counter.

Not fast enough, he thought at me.

"I should be, if I were true to my heritage," he said out loud. "We're on the same side, Molly."

"I'm not even positive that I believe demons exist at all," I said.

"Yet, here I am," he said. We sat in silence for a few

minutes while I tried to absorb what he was saying.

"So, demons are real. What else?"

"What do you mean?" He crossed his arms over his chest and looked at me. He seemed to fill my kitchen. The amount of power emanating from him, washing over me was insane. I really, really disliked that.

"Well, if demons are real, what about vampires? Werewolves, ghosts, fairies?"

He snorted. "Fairies?"

"I'm asking you. Are they real?"

"We have things called sprites. I guess they're similar to your fairies," he said thoughtfully. "They're vicious little shits, though."

I nodded. "Okay." Took a breath. "Anything else?"

He leaned forward. "Name your nightmare, Molly. Vampires, weres, zombies, witches….all of them walk the streets of this city just as you do."

"How come I haven't come across them?"

"How do you know you haven't? You've been around. Undoubtedly seen shit that can't be explained."

"People will do horrendous things to each other. No supernatural help is required for that," I said, trying to ignore the way my skin prickled, the way my pulse raced, from his power surrounding me.

"Yeah. But a whisper from a demon, a spell from a witch… those things can help it along."

We sat in silence for several long moments. He was tense. I would have known that without the ability to read emotions; the man was coiled like a spring, ready to strike at a moment. I had the feeling he probably felt like this even when he was asleep. I knew I did.

"So… a demon," I said finally. "Surprisingly, that doesn't make me feel any better about you."

"I didn't expect to have to tell you right away. It only makes it harder, once people know what I am."

"Well, to be fair, I didn't trust you anyway," I muttered, and he let out a short laugh. More uncomfortable silence.

"So how did it come about?" I asked, more to break the silence than anything else.

"What?"

"The decision to ignore what you are and fight for the good guys instead."

I felt some irritation, uncertainty coming from him. Now that Nain was sitting in my well-lit kitchen, I could see that he had tattoos that went from under his t-shirt, up one side of his neck. Both forearms were covered in them. Symbols I wasn't familiar with, in black. He didn't look like a three hundred year old demon. He looked like a thirty-something athlete. Maybe a football player.

"For the first half of my life, I was a typical demon," he said. He met my eyes. "I did all the things my kind do. Kill, torture, rape…none of it was out of bounds."

I felt a little sick. Watched him. He continued.

"Then, I was rampaging one night, and I came upon this house. Family. I killed the father. Went after the baby, while the mother screamed and fought me with every bit of strength she had. Something clicked. That's the only way to explain it," he paused, thinking. "What I was doing was wrong. It was who I was, what I knew, but it was wrong. So I left, and I vowed that I wouldn't cause harm again."

He met my eyes. "The problem with that, is that demons need fear. We need pain. It's sustenance to us." I could barely breathe.

He went on. "Once you stop causing fear and pain, you grow weak. And then other demons can make an easy hunt of you." He paused. "The good thing is that fear is fear, no matter who it's coming from. Going after the murderers and rapists, taking down my fellow demons, it all fed me just as much as killing innocents. And, after a hundred years or so, I could look at myself in the mirror again."

"So, you still feed off of pain and terror, even now?"

He nodded. "Even now. It's like lust. You can't even

put it on the same level as just 'hunger.' No amount is ever enough. There is no sense of fullness. I just want more and more, all the time."

I felt my stomach clench. "Have you ever been tempted to hurt an innocent, since then?"

He shook his head. "There are more than enough assholes out there to keep me busy. And I feel good about causing them pain."

I nodded. "I think I know how you feel."

"Yeah. You seem to enjoy your work. Some of the beatings I've seen you give have been pretty magnificent."

I sat, looking at Nain. Felt a jumble of emotions from him. "You're uncertain about me," I said, finally.

"Stay out of my emotions," he told me, and I felt irritation roll off of him.

"I can't help it," I said. "They're just there. I can't turn it off. And believe me, I've spent years trying."

"It's a rare ability. It must be difficult to live with," he said.

"Sometimes, yeah. When I was a teenager, I started realizing what I was feeling. It was a lifesaver, because up until that point, I was convinced that I was going insane. I'd be walking and all of a sudden feel like ripping someone's throat out, or I'd be reading in school and suddenly feel ridiculously happy. I didn't know what was wrong with me."

"You learned to deal with it," he said.

"Mostly by refusing to feel anything," I said. "Over the years, I've just kind of learned to deaden myself to all emotions. Mine, others." We sat in silence for a few minutes. "That's a large part of why I don't want any part of this team you keep talking about. And, I don't trust you, and I know that you don't trust me."

He looked at me. "Not entirely. The stuff you can do….you don't even know what you're capable of yet. If you don't get some training, if you don't have people you can talk to, you could cause a lot of problems. You can make bad things happen, and you have no idea how bad you could be."

He paused, took a breath. "I can feel power just rolling off of you. I've never felt so much power in one person. If you went bad, there would be hell to pay. For everyone." *And I don't want to be the one that has to take you down,* he thought at me, as if unwilling to say the words out loud.

I have no intention of going bad, Nain.

I don't think most people intend for it to happen. It just happens. One moment, one action at a time, until the bad things outweigh the good.

I thought about that for a minute. Sighed. "I know I need to shield my thoughts. Meeting you has made that abundantly clear." I shook my head, wondered what the hell I was getting myself into. "If you'd teach me that, I'd appreciate it. As for the rest," I said, shrugging. "I don't think I'm quite super hero squad material."

He nodded, standing up. Apparently, we were finished here. I got up and led him back through the living room to the front door.

I stepped out onto the porch and he stood beside me. The night air was still humid, sultry. It was quiet, except for the crickets and the occasional dog barking in the distance. "So, when do we start?" I finally asked, looking up at him. It felt like a noose was starting to tighten around my neck. I bit my lip, trying to hold my irritation in check.

"We can start tomorrow, if you want. Meet me at Eastern Market around eight. We can have breakfast. Good to practice in a crowded place," he explained when I was about to complain.

"Fine. Farmer's Restaurant?"

He nodded.

I nodded back to him. "All right. I'll see you then," I said stepping toward the door. Then I turned back around, watched him heading for his truck. "Hey, Nain," I said.

He turned. "What?"

"I'm putting a level of trust in you that I'm not feeling comfortable with. Give me a reason to regret it, and I will absolutely follow through on that threat I made earlier about turning your balls into earrings."

He nodded. "Understood." And then he got into his truck and roared away, and I rolled my eyes and asked myself for the thousandth time what the hell I was getting myself into.

I laid in bed for hours, staring up at the ceiling. The branches of the humongous oak tree outside cast shadows, and I watched them dance in the soft breeze. My bedroom, usually so comforting, didn't offer much solace. The antique quilt, the vintage alarm clock with its glow-in-the-dark face, the kitschy McCoy planters spilling over with succulents on the plant stand by the window – none of it made me feel relaxed or safe. Not the way it usually did. I tried not to think of the night I'd had. Of those guns pointed point-blank at my face. Of the whole Nain situation. Of what he'd said about how bad things could be if I turned.

I don't want to be the one that has to take you down.

Acknowledgment, in that simple thought, that he didn't want to, that he wouldn't like it, but that he'd do it. No question about it.

I didn't trust him. But, at the same time, it was a relief to have someone know what I was. Who knew that I was a person beyond the "Angel" persona the media had created. Made me feel almost real. The thing was, I wanted to trust him.

And that could be more dangerous than even a dozen guns pointed at my face.

I glanced at the clock. Almost three AM. I turned over onto my side, punching my pillow for good measure. And heard the light tinkle of glass breaking somewhere down below.

CHAPTER FOUR

I got out of bed and tiptoed toward the stairs, avoiding all of the places where the floorboards creaked. Down the stairs, and I could see a light on in the kitchen.

What kind of asshole burglar turns the light on?

I walked into the kitchen, to see a woman sitting at the kitchen table, looking thoughtfully at the fruit magnets on the refrigerator. At least, that's what I thought she was looking at.

She looked like a kindergarten teacher. Curly blond hair. Blue eyes. A long flowing skirt and white polo shirt. She even had a dimple when she smiled at me, for Christ sake.

I didn't like her. At all.

The feelings coming from the woman were nothing good. Anger, haughtiness, superiority. I wondered for a minute if she was crazy. She could have been. But she was also evil. I could just feel the sliminess emanating from her. I rubbed my hands on my pajama pants, feeling dirty just by being in the same room.

"Well, why don't you make yourself at home? Can I get you a cup of tea? Sandwich, maybe?" I asked, strolling toward the table and leaning on the back of one of the chairs.

"Sarcasm doesn't suit you, dear," the woman said.

"Who are you, and what are you doing here?" I asked, power filling my voice.

"Ah ah ah. That doesn't work on me. Impressive, though," the woman said, shaking her finger in a way that made me want to rip it off and shove it down her throat.

"Then I'll ask a second time. Who are you? What are you doing here? Don't make me ask again." I could hear the snarl in my voice, could feel my power spiking.

MY damn house. The one place in the whole city where I could catch a break. And this slimy bitch was sitting in it. I glared at her.

"Manners, manners," the woman said. "Really, I'm not surprised. Rude child," she muttered. "I am known as the Puppeteer. I have a proposition for you."

I laughed. "The Puppeteer? Seriously? Someone's been reading too many 1960s comic books."

"It's the only name that matters," the woman snapped. "As I was saying, I have a proposition for you." She smoothed her skirt and folded her hands delicately in her lap.

"So, spit it out."

"We will have to work on your manners. Come and work with me. I could use someone with your talents. You would be shocked at the amount of power available to you."

I took a deep breath. Despite my wisecracking, this woman made me feel physically ill. "I work alone. Not a team player. And I'm not all that power-hungry right now, thanks."

"I won't make this offer again. Perhaps I need to be more persuasive," she said softly, appraisingly, in a voice that chilled me through and through. I was about to tell her where to shove it, when I felt an oiliness invade my mind.

"Oh, delicious," the woman purred. And I was flooded

with visions I'd spent most of my life trying to forget.

Basement. Pain. Darkness. Flames. Blood.

Despite the vileness I was reliving, I could hear the Puppeteer sighing in what could only be described as ecstasy. "Oh, how very interesting," the woman moaned.

And all I could feel was a filth, a greasiness, writhing through my mind. Dread filled me. Fear. Overwhelming terror. Hatred. Everything was so intense, it made me dizzy and nauseous.

I gagged. The visions stopped, almost as if they'd never been there at all.

"Join me," the woman purred, and the sound of her voice, like she'd just finished eating the world's most satisfying meal, was sickening.

I took deep breaths. My legs wanted to collapse under me. Here's the thing: I fucking *hate* feeling weak. I Hulk-smashed my way through life, mostly to avoid having that feeling ever again.

And I had just gone from merely annoyed to flat-out enraged.

The hatred I had for the woman sitting in my kitchen was stronger than my fear, at least for now.

"Time to bleed," I muttered, lunging across the table and throwing a hard right cross at the Puppeteer's (seriously, how ridiculous is that name?) face. It dropped the woman to the floor, and when she got up, I was on her, hit her with a left, knocking her back into the table. A cup and a vase fell off the table, crashed to the floor. I kicked out, caught her in the stomach. The Puppeteer bent double, then recovered just enough to throw a coffee cup from the kitchen sink at me, and I ducked, snarled. It was just enough time for the bitch to make a mad dash for the open side door, and she was out, running into the night. I followed, sprinting as fast as I could. My bare feet hit stones, broken glass, but I kept running, the Puppeteer just a few houses ahead of me, glancing back with a look of "oh, shit" on her face every few seconds. It would have been funny if I didn't still feel her slime all over my psyche.

I put on a final burst of speed. Running had never been my strong point. I usually just smashed.

I almost had her. Almost. And then a car pulled up and the Puppeteer jumped into the passenger seat.

She glared out at me, nose bleeding profusely onto her perfect white shirt, I noted with more than a little satisfaction. "I don't give second chances. Go, you idiot!" she shrieked at the driver. Then the car squealed away and I was left on the corner, trying to catch my breath. I bent over, resting my hands on my knees. Shook my head.

After a few seconds of sucking wind, I limped back to my house. I really did need to take up running. Somewhere in all my free time, I guess.

My feet stung. They'd heal, but it hurt like hell. I tried not to think about what the Puppeteer had forced me to see, but images swam before my eyes, the types of things I lived over and over again in nightmares.

I got back, walked in the side door, and locked up. I'd have to get the window fixed. More damn money I didn't have.

I plopped down at the kitchen table, took a look at my feet. One large shard of jagged glass protruded from my heel. I grasped it and pulled it out, gritting my teeth against the pain. The bleeding stopped as the gash closed up. I put my elbows on the table and rested my head in my hands. Looked at the broken coffee cup on the floor.

"Bitch broke my Jadeite," I muttered to the now-empty kitchen. "She's gonna pay for that." I sat there until the sun came up, staring at the floor, afraid to focus on anything else.

CHAPTER FIVE

I showed up at Farmer's Restaurant a little after eight. After the night I'd had, the last thing I wanted to do was sit and chit-chat with Nain, have him poking around in my mind. I felt nauseous, still slimy, reliving the Puppeteer's invasion of my memories.

I walked into the restaurant, looked around, and spotted Nain in a booth across the room. A waitress came to seat me, and I pointed to Nain, headed to the table where he was sitting. He stood up as I approached.

I sat down and ordered coffee, and Nain settled back into his seat. The aromas of coffee and frying bacon, usually two of the best scents on the planet, were doing a number on my stomach. I swallowed and tried to ignore them.

"Have you been here before?" he asked, and I got the sense, somehow, that he was making an effort to be sociable.

I nodded. "Yes, a few times. Good pancakes," I said, messing with the green Jade ring on my right index finger.

"Jade?" he asked, gesturing at the ring. I nodded.

So, awkward silences were apparently our specialty. The waitress brought my coffee, refilled his, and took our order. Then we sat there for a few more minutes of awkward silence. Well. I felt awkward. He just seemed patient. Unnaturally patient. It was annoying. I looked at the sign on the wall next to our booth. "We're a few eggs short of a dozen!" it said. Yeah.

"Rough night?" Nain finally asked.

I took a sip of my coffee, after mixing in plenty of sugar and creamer. "You could say that," I muttered.

"What's wrong?"

I shook my head. "I had a visitor last night," I said finally. "Someone broke into my house around three."

He was quiet a minute. I wondered if he was reading my thoughts. *Fuck you*, I thought at him. No response at all from him.

Finally, he said, "Are you okay?"

I shrugged. "Sure." I took another sip of coffee. "Have you ever heard of someone calling herself the Puppeteer?"

"Yes. We've come up against her and her little army a few times. She is vile," he said, and the disdain in his voice made me smile a little.

"Yeah. Vile is a good word," I said.

"You mean she was the one who broke into your house? Not one of her puppets?"

"I had the pleasure of meeting her face to face," I said. "What's her story?"

"She takes people. Erases their thoughts and memories. And then she uses them for muscle for her crime syndicate. She's into all kinds of evil. Drugs. Human trafficking, prostitution. Her puppets are a thoughtless, perfectly-programmed defense force."

"Who does she take?"

"Whoever she can. She seems to prefer them big and strong. She prefers that they already know how to shoot or kill. Less training required that way," Nain finished, watching me. "What happened, Molls?"

I raised my eyebrow at the nickname, shook my head. "She had a business proposition for me." I fiddled with the sugar packets on the table between us. "Join her.

Unlimited power and luxury. Be her second in command. Own this city. Blah, blah."

"You said no."

"Obviously," I said, glaring at him. "She wasn't happy about that."

"What happened?" he asked.

I was silent for a few seconds. Remembering. Then I shrugged. "She tried to be more persuasive," was all I finally said.

I felt something in my mind, and realized Nain was in there. I stood up. "That's it. I told you to stay out of my thoughts. This was a bad idea. I'm not a people person. Just stay the hell away from me." And then I left, stalking out and slamming the door open hard as I left the restaurant.

Violation. Theft. Assault by psychic methods. That's exactly what that was, and I felt my power spike with my rage. I stalked toward my car, my power practically burning through me, and I snarled when I heard heavy footsteps behind me.

"Molly," Nain shouted, running to catch up with me. I walked faster. So did he.

He closed in on me, reached out and grabbed my elbow.

I don't think I planned what happened next.

I turned, and rewarded Nain with a growl and a blast of pure energy that sent him across the service drive and slammed him into the chain-link uprights on the bridge.

Oh, shit.

Well. He did have it coming.

I took a second to watch him pulling himself out of the mangled chain link. And he was pissed. Royally, royally pissed. My rage still burned within me, and his washed over me just as strongly. *I did tell you to stay out of my thoughts,* I thought at him.

I jogged to my car, got in. Sat there, trying to breathe. "What the ever-loving fuck was that?" I asked the empty car. I could feel myself starting to panic, feel my power spiking again.

It hurt. I gritted my teeth against it. And of course, just then, the son of a bitch was knocking on my window. I snarled, pushed the door open.

He towered over me, three hundred pounds of very pissed, very powerful demon. "Explain," he said, and it sounded as if it was taking him some effort to control himself. This wasn't gonna be good.

I could feel my power building within me, burning hotter in response to his anger, my own fright. It happened sometimes, when I was very emotional, and being near him just seemed to magnify everything. I glanced up at Nain, and I could tell from the way he positioned his body, defensive, that he felt it, too.

"I felt you in my mind, again," I said, aware of the threat in my voice.

He just looked at me, seething.

"I told you to stay out. Between you and the Puppeteer, I have had entirely too many people violating my conscience in the last day or so."

I felt a tiny bit of guilt from him, but not much. "What did she do to you?"

"She dug out some old shit I've been trying to bury. Turned my thoughts against me," I finished, hating the tremor in my voice. "I couldn't even move. I was just stuck there." I hated remembering that feeling of absolute helplessness. I'd spent my entire adult life doing what I could to avoid feeling that, ever again. I balled my hands into fists as my power surged.

"So did she just decide to leave or what?" Nain asked finally, nervousness from him.

I looked at a spot just over his shoulder. "After she was done, she made her offer again. And it just pissed me off."

"And?" Nain asked.

"I punched her in the face. Twice."

Nain let out a short laugh. I felt his rage dial back, just

a little. "I never would have thought of that," he said.

"I wasn't thinking. I just wanted to hit her. Hard. Anyway, after a few hits, she ran for it. I chased her about a block, determined to hit her some more. But she had a car waiting."

We stood, leaning against the side of my car. I took deep breaths, trying to draw down my power. He looked at me. "That still doesn't explain your reaction to me," he said quietly. "What the hell was that?"

"I was going to ask you the same thing," I muttered.

"That's never happened before?"

I shook my head. "I can't turn it down. I had so much power built up in me, and it just blasted like that…that was nuts. And I am loaded up again, and how do I avoid blasting the shit out of someone? What if I hurt someone? What if I'd blasted some innocent pedestrian instead of your infuriating ass?"

"It's not the first time I've seen someone do that." I sensed apprehension from him, something else I couldn't quite pinpoint. "You need training."

"I do not want you messing around in my head."

"It's the only way. I'll promise to stay out unless I tell you I'm going in first. And I'll only go in when we're training."

I was quiet. My power had receded again. Relief. "This seems unlike you," I finally said.

"Meaning?"

"You seem like a pushy, entitled, take-what-you-want asshole. Why are you giving in so easily?" I looked over at him, met his eyes.

"Right on all counts."

"So?"

"One: you need to train. I don't want distrust of me standing in the way of that. Two: that fucking *hurt*, Molly. Damn."

I bit my lip, trying not to laugh. I hated him. I really, really could not stand him.

Unfortunately, he was my only chance to get my powers under control and my mind protected from the Puppeteer and anyone like her.

"Yeah, Okay." I finally said. "But I'm still not super hero squad material."

"Okay. You want to practice now?"

I looked at my watch, shook my head. "I'm already late for work," I said. One more irritation. Blasting my boss like that would be a really bad move, too.

"All right." He wrote something down. "This is my cell number, the phone number and address at the loft. Soon, Molls," he said; an order. I just glared at him, giving his back the evil eye as he walked away.

Two days and about two dozen nagging/threatening text messages from Nain later, I gave in and headed to the address Nain had given me. I pulled into parking garage below what looked like an old warehouse. Expensive part of town, nowadays, between Midtown and Downtown. Something told me Nain had owned the building long before the recent real estate boom in this area.

I got out of the car and walked toward an elevator. It was one of those kind of old-fashioned elevators with a gate that you pull down instead of solid doors. The way it creaked its way down when I pushed the button made me wish for stairs.

And, just my luck, Nain had decided to play welcoming crew. I could feel him before the elevator creaked down to my level, before I got a glimpse of his brown hiking boots, then jean-clad legs, then t-shirted torso. And then there was the ever-present glare he gave me when his face did finally come into sight.

When the elevator squeaked to a stop, he lifted the gate and I got in. He closed it, hit the button to take us back up. "It's a good time to get acquainted. Everyone's here, and we're meeting about some intel we just received." I nodded, and we rode the rest of the way up in silence. I was more nervous than I'd been about anything in a long time. That was irritating. After everything I'd been through, what the hell did I have to be nervous about now?

"Because you're about to meet a whole group of people like yourself, people with power," Nain said. "Your eyes are about to get opened, Molls."

"Stay out of my mind," I muttered.

"Learn to shield it, and I won't be able to hear you," Nain said. The elevator came to a stop, and he opened the door. We walked into a little foyer-type area, with a large oak door ahead of us. Nain opened it, waved me through. I stepped in and looked around. Someone was doing very, very well for himself. The loft was spacious. Full of natural light and soaring ceilings. Expensive leather furniture in the living room, which was situated near a wall of windows looking out over the Cultural Center. A kitchen with granite counter tops and dark wood cabinets was on the other side of the loft, along with what looked like a small office area. Most of the loft was empty, and mahogany floors gleamed. Two sets of stairs, one at each end of the loft, led to a second level, to what I guessed were bedrooms, bathrooms.

I could have spent more time admiring the (very expensive) decor, but the group of people sitting in the living room caught my attention. Really, they were impossible to ignore. They all looked up as the door opened, and every one of their gazes landed solidly on me. I steeled myself. I was a total badass, right? The Angel, finder of lost girls. Right.

The expressions on their faces ranged from shock to curiosity to distrust. I felt all of that, and something that felt like active dislike, coming from the group of six powerful beings staring at me.

Nain started walking toward them, and I had no choice but to follow. To be fair, I did consider bolting for the door. But that seemed undignified.

"You have something, Ada?" Nain asked as he approached the group.

The middle-aged black woman sitting on the sofa nodded, dragged her gaze away from me. "We know where he's going to be tomorrow night. It's not going to be easy, though." She looked at me again, and I forced myself to meet her gaze. No showing weakness, not now. Ada transferred her gaze to another man, and I followed it. The man was staring at me.

"Hello, Angel," the man said, warmth in his voice. He was probably around fifty, bald, and built like a brick shithouse (as one of my foster fathers had liked to say) – solid, huge. He wore a leather biker jacket and jeans. Work boots on his feet and a white mustache on his face.

I just nodded. Felt like if I opened my mouth, I'd puke. Definitely undignified. I could feel the power swirling in this room. Nain's was strongest, and then one of the men, then Ada, then the biker guy, then the others. Emotions ran strong here, a stampede. It was very close to overwhelming me. This was one of the many reasons I avoided groups of people. Too loud, too emotional, too everything. I took a deep breath, worked at deadening myself against their emotions a little. Not completely; I'd still know what they were feeling. But enough so that their emotions didn't have such a punch to them. Not easy, but it was something I'd been doing for a long time. A few seconds later, and I had managed to deaden their emotions to a dull roar.

Nain was standing next to me. "Everyone, I'd like you to meet Molly Brooks. Molly, this is the team. Stone," he said, gesturing to the biker guy. "Brennan," pointing at a thirty-something with dirty blond, longish hair and a five-o'clock shadow. "George and Veronica," he said, pointing to the couple on the loveseat. "And Ada," gesturing to the woman who'd been observing me.

"A pleasure to meet the finder of lost girls," Stone said to me, still watching me closely, as if trying to place me.

"She's more than that," the blond guy, Brennan, said. "She's powerful." He looked at me. "What can you do?"

I felt curiosity, respect coming from him. It made me wonder if there was a social order among those with powers the way there was among animals. This man reminded me of a wild animal, a predator. Something in his eyes, in the way even the smallest movements looked controlled and deadly.

I glanced at Nain. He met my eyes and nodded.

I took a breath. "I can read thoughts. Sense emotions." I looked at Nain again, and he nodded for me to go on.

All of it, Molls, he thought at me.

"I can take memories, plant things that weren't there. I can make people act against their will." I felt a torrent of emotion, most of it dread, coming from the rest of the people in the room. I gritted my teeth against it.

"And I can self-heal," I finished. And a storm of emotions — shock, disbelief –hit me, all at once.

Stay strong. I can imagine what you're feeling from them.

Uh, yeah.

I forced myself to look at them. The man and woman on the couch looked as if they were looking at a cobra that was getting ready to strike. Ada looked thoughtful. I looked back at the man who had asked the question in the first place. Saw open admiration, curiosity on his face.

"But that's not the only way you rescue lost girls," he said, standing up and walking toward me. "I've heard the stories. About a tiny woman who pounds much bigger men into oblivion. Broken knees, broken noses. I heard about a time you broke all of the bones in a guy's hand, just because he was being uncooperative. Was that true?" By now, he had reached me, and was practically circling me, like a dog getting ready to fight. "Or was it all bullshit?"

"Do you want to find out?" I muttered, meeting his blue eyes.

He smiled, a flash of perfect white teeth. "I thought

you'd never ask."

Brennan gave a small bow and motioned for me to head to the open part of the loft.

"Are you sure you want to do this?" Nain asked.

"Of course," I said, glancing at him.

Nain smiled. "I wasn't talking to you, Molls."

I bit back the grin forming on my lips, glanced at Brennan. I reached what I now realized was the training floor — a punching bag was in one corner, and weapons hung on one of the walls. I turned, ready. Brennan stood there, stripped off his shirt and threw it off to the side, revealing the hard, muscled body of someone who clearly did this kind of thing a lot. A long scar slashed across his ribcage.

"Rules?" I asked.

"No punching in the face. No mind control bullshit. Other than that, use what ya got. Time to see if you're as batshit insane as I think you are." I nodded. Stood ready. He grinned. "So, how should I kick your ass? As a man or as a beast?"

I was confused for a second, then I realized what he was saying: shapeshifter. Oh, hell. I gave him a bored glance, trying to look much calmer than I actually was. "You do whatever you feel you need to do," I said.

He lunged for me, and I deflected. He tried to grab my arm, and I twisted out of it effortlessly. I punched, landed one to his abdomen. He shook it off, lunged for me again, knocked me down with a hard kick to my abdomen. I landed and rolled away, bounced up again. I kicked out, landed a solid kick right to his knee, and he fell hard, then sprung up as a tiger, roared at me.

Oh, shit.

I spun, kicked the tiger in the face and sent it flying back into the wall. He changed form again, into a grizzly bear, thundered at me, took a swipe with a clawed paw. I ducked, he lunged again. I could see Nain and the rest of the group all watching tensely. I landed a kick to the chest that sent the bear down on its back, but it came up, lunged at me, and I evaded.

This went on for what seemed like forever.

It landed a smack with its giant paw that sent me crashing into the wall, then it came at me again. I kicked out with both feet and all my power, sent him flying across most of the loft.

"Holy shit," Stone muttered. Veronica gasped.

And he changed form again, into a man, and he came at me with a knife.

"Not fair," I gasped. The muscles in my arms and legs were burning. I was sore, but healing. What the hell had I been thinking?

"Like I said, use what ya got," Brennan said, equally out of breath but grinning as if he was having an absolute blast.

We fought, hand to hand, both of us breathing hard. He was a flurry of movement that I was having a harder and harder time tracking. I swatted the knife aside several times, got a cut across one arm, and he still kept coming. I kicked, hard, at his groin, but he deflected, laughing as he did it. He landed a few solid punches to my stomach. And I landed just as many.

Then I feinted, making like I was going to punch him again, and instead kicked him, low, sweeping his feet out from under him. He laid there, started to reach for me, and before I could back off, he had me, and we wrestled in earnest. After a while, it felt like my strength was going to give out. Finally, with one last twist, and a good dose of my power to back me up, I got him down, held his arm twisted behind him.

"Give up?" I asked him, barely able to speak.

Quicker than I would have guessed, he reached up, grabbed me by the hair and threw me to the floor. Then he straddled me, held me down by the throat. His grip was steel, and he was completely unmoved by the way I bucked my body and clawed at his arms, drawing blood.

"Never underestimate your opponent," he said, his voice like a low growl. "Taking the time to gloat after you think you've won only opens you up for retaliation. Remember that." He released me and stood up. He pulled his shirt back on (covering the many bruises I'd given him, I noted with some satisfaction) and then came back and held out a hand, which I took grudgingly, and he pulled me up.

He grinned at me. I had misjudged this one. He played the goofball, the flirt. He was freaking terrifying. I glared at him. I am not a good loser. Whatever.

"Sorry about those kicks to the groin," I said, stepping back from him.

He was still grinning. "It's all right. Sorry about the hair pulling. That must have hurt." He looked at me appreciatively, and I felt respect coming from him. "By the way, you are batshit insane."

I laughed. Turned to see Nain watching us with an unreadable look in his eyes. Annoyance rolled off of him.

Just then, the door buzzer rang.

"That would be the pizza," Stone said, getting up from his chair. "You came just in time for lunch," he said to me, smiling.

Over slices of the best pizza I'd ever had, the team filled me in on powers. Veronica could kill with a touch, thanks to some kind of neurotoxin that she secreted in her body and could call at will. George could turn himself and anyone or anything he was touching invisible. Stone was ridiculously strong.

"I've seen him push over entire brick buildings without even getting out of breath," Nain told me, taking a bite of pizza.

"Remember that time he knocked down the wall of the loft?" Ada asked, laughing. It was one of those rich, infectious laughs that made me smile along with her.

"I thought Nain was going to go all demon on me. Those were the good old days," Stone said, laughing so hard he started choking on his pizza. The rest of the group laughed, and Nain patted him hard on the back.

The laughter died down, and Ada looked at me, a smile in her eyes. "So, are you with us?" she asked.

"What's your thing?" I asked. Avoid the question by asking a question. It was my signature move.

"Witchcraft. And intelligence. I'm the eyes and ears."

"Witchcraft?" I said. "Is that even real?"

Ada raised her eyebrows. "You control people's thoughts. You fought a shapeshifter today. You're asking me if witchcraft is real?"

I shrugged.

"Besides, I assumed you were a practitioner already," Ada continued.

"Why?"

"That jade ring on your finger. You know what jade is for, right?"

I shook my head.

"It helps heal the self, wards off negative energies. It's a decent defensive gem."

"I just bought it because it's pretty," I said.

"You should learn some witchcraft, girl," Ada said.

"Here she goes, pushing the witchcraft again," Stone said, laughing. Ada shushed him.

I shook my head.

"You can also use it to fight, you know," Ada said, smiling.

"Really?"

"Of course. It's not all gems and potions. Though I've found those things to be imminently useful in my experience. If you can control your will, you'd be surprised at what you can do in a fight."

"Such as?"

"Using your will, rather than your body, to push back an opponent. Being able to bind someone."

"I can already bind, by telling them not to move," I pointed out.

"But what if you come up against someone that won't work on? Like Nain? Or the Puppeteer? That wouldn't work against them, because they are telepaths like you."

"You're saying telepathic powers negate each other," I said.

Ada nodded. The rest of the team was quiet, listening to our exchange. I could feel Nain's eyes on me, sense the tension coming from him. It made me want to grit my teeth. From my limited knowledge of him, he was always like this. It exhausted me, just being near him. I glanced back up at Ada.

"So why did the Puppeteer's work on me?"

Ada opened her mouth, closed it. Looked at Nain. "I don't know."

Nain met my eyes. "I suspect she has a few witches on her team. Some of the things she can do don't make any sense, as far as telepaths go. Her associates have witches and warlocks on the payroll. No reason to think she hasn't followed suit."

I nodded.

"Which brings us to the reason I brought Molly here. She needs some training, and I'm going to do what I can to help her."

"So you're not joining the team?" Brennan asked, disappointed.

I shook my head. "I'm not really a team type of person."

"You're kidding," he said, looking at Nain. "You're not just going to accept that, are you? Jesus, man, the power coming off of her. We need her."

"We've been over it. She works alone." Nain shrugged.

"Then why did you bring her here?" George asked. It was the first time he'd spoken the entire time, and he had a high-pitched, wavery voice that I found irritating. "She shouldn't be here if she's not on the team. How do we know where her loyalties lie?"

Stone, who was sitting next to George, smacked the

young man in the back of his head, not gently. "If Nain and Brennan trust her, that's enough." I looked at the older man, then glanced at Brennan, who had been watching me. He winked at me, and I looked away. These people were all fucking insane.

"No, it's a valid question," Nain said, holding his hands up. "She needs training, and this is the best place to do that. Free of distractions. She can come and go as she pleases."

Everyone watched me. "I really didn't want to be brought here or get involved with any of you. Nain is a stubborn pain in the ass," I said, giving him a bit of stink-eye for good measure.

Brennan laughed, Stone guffawed, and everyone else looked at me in surprise. Clearly, Nain ran a tight ship. Not used to being questioned. I'd be damned if I was going to 'yes, sir' or 'no, sir' Nain. No way.

"Well, I'm hoping to change her mind about joining up," Nain said. "We can't make her do anything she doesn't want to do. And pity the fool who tried," he muttered under his breath. Brennan laughed.

"What does she need training in? Maybe we can help," Veronica said.

"Shielding."

"Oh."

"She also has some control issues that we're going to be working on."

"Uh, control issues? I have to ask again, especially considering how much power she can throw around, was it really a smart idea to bring her here?" George asked, and he turned abruptly to Stone. "And if you hit me in the head, I will make sure you never find your motorcycle again, old man."

Stone just grinned.

Nain cleared his throat. I could feel irritation coming from him. "You don't need to worry about it," he said.

"She could probably use a sparring partner every once

in a while too," Brennan said, looking at me and smiling.

Nain nodded. "Probably. Between the two of us, she'll get plenty of combat practice."

"Hey, wait. I never agreed to that," I said, glaring at Nain.

"You want to work solo? Fine. But I'm going to make damn sure that you learn everything you need to to keep yourself and everyone else safe." Steel in his tone, determination washing over me like a wave.

That was when I realized that I was utterly and completely screwed.

Once the team started to disperse, leaving to do whatever it is a super hero squad of freaks do, Nain and I wandered up onto the roof of his building. I looked around. There was a wrought-iron table and chairs. Barbecue grill. Three wooden lounge chairs, painted bright red, and an old-fashioned metal glider. The view was fantastic, overlooking the Detroit Institute of Arts and the campus of Wayne State University, which looked much prettier from this vantage point than it did when I was at work there. Downtown glittered not too far in the distance in the opposite direction. We stood in silence for a while.

"I don't think the crew is especially fond of me," I finally said.

"Does it matter?" Nain asked, leaning against the low wall that surrounded the roof deck.

I shrugged.

"Brennan likes you. Stone and Ada think you're all right."

I could feel Nain's eyes on me. Felt empty and just generally off-balance under his gaze. "And George and Veronica look at me like I'm about to sprout horns or something."

"They're the weakest among us. Easily threatened. You could have come in looking like Glinda the good witch or something and they still would have been terrified of you. It's as it should be."

I didn't respond. Didn't know why it even mattered to me. I stared out over the city, needing to ask Nain something, knowing I wouldn't want to hear the answer. He stood, as always, silent, watching, tense. Waiting.

"So, Brennan's a shifter. Ada's a witch. George, Veronica, and Stone are all basically Normals with a power thrown into the mix."

He nodded.

"I recognized Brennan and Ada's power signatures. I've come across similar ones before and just didn't know it. Didn't know what to look for."

"Yeah. That's part of the reason I wanted you to meet everyone. It's not possible to be around as much crazy shit as you have and not come across something like us."

I took a breath. "So I know what they are. And I know what you are." I paused. "What the hell am I?" I asked quietly. I couldn't look at him, kept my eyes glued to a skyscraper in the distance. He was tense, something else. He was harder to read than most.

"I think you already know," he finally said. "You don't need me to tell you." I closed my eyes.

"My power has a weird response to you."

"Yeah."

"I get stronger the more pain I cause."

"Yeah."

I finally turned and looked at him. "How is that even possible? How?"

"Demons spawn just like anyone else. A boy demon and girl demon got together…."

"Oh, shut up," I muttered. He laughed.

"This is so messed up."

"I'm not telling you anything you didn't already suspect. I knew it the second I first saw you." He paused. "There's something off about you, though."

"You're just now figuring this out?" I asked, sitting down on one of the lounge chairs.

"Your power feels off, I mean."

"How?"

He paused, thinking. "You're incredibly strong. Probably stronger than I am. Fifty years ago or so, when I still had my demonic form, I was much stronger than I am now. You still could have flattened me, even back then."

"What happened to your demon form?" I asked.

He gave me a sharp look. "Not now."

I raised my eyebrow. *Hit a sore spot, did I?*

He ignored me. "What I'm saying is, you're one of the most powerful demons I've ever met. But there's something more to you, something else."

"So I'm not a hundred percent demon? Maybe one of my parents is a witch or something?"

He shrugged. "Or something. It doesn't feel like witch either."

"Well this has been really helpful," I said, rolling my eyes. Felt irritation, impatience spike from him.

"It is very easy to get under your skin, you know that?" I asked.

He glared at me. "No. You're just a very irritating woman."

"What's your name?" I asked him.

"What the hell is with the change in subject? And I told you my name." Irritation, again.

"Your real name. We both know Nain is from what the Normals started calling you with all of that Nain Rouge stuff. What's your name, really?"

He snorted. "You think I'm going to give you my real name? Names have power in our world."

"The freak world?"

"The demon world."

"You know my real name," I pointed out.

"No. And neither do you," he said.

I looked at him, waiting. He huffed, impatient. "The name your real parents gave you. Whatever they called you when you spawned. That's your real name. And since you don't know them, you have no idea what they named you.

You have the name the Normals gave you. It's not who you really are."

Silence stretched between us. Nain finally broke it. "We should probably practice shielding a little before you leave."

I nodded.

He sat, cross legged, on the ground, waved me over. I came and sat the same way across from him. Our knees almost touched.

"Is it essential to sit like this?" I asked.

"No, but this way I'm close enough to reach you if you need to be physically controlled."

I glared at him.

"Not that I'm expecting that to be an issue."

"Of course," I said.

"Okay. Close your eyes," he said.

I'm going to try to get into your mind, I don't know what I'll see. What I see is between the two of us. His voice in my mind.

"Stop. I don't want to do this." I started to get up. He reached out and held onto my wrist, preventing me from moving. His touch made me shiver, made something inside me rise in excitement. I tried to ignore it.

"Molls. Trust me. There's nothing I'll see there that can make me think less of you. Anything you've done, I've done worse."

"It's not the things I've done that I'm worried about you seeing," I said, wrenching my wrist back. He let me go.

I met his eyes.

Trust me.

I gave a small nod, closed my eyes again. I felt a warmth, a strong presence that I now recognized as uniquely Nain. It felt very different from the way the Puppeteer had felt, with her slick, oily presence.

I focused on keeping my mind blank, withstanding having him there at the periphery of my psyche. It made me feel sick, went against every instinct I had to keep my barriers intact.

Okay. Picture whatever you need to as a shield for your mind. Some people picture a wall, or a safe, or something like that. Picture it, make it real.

I focused. A steel box, impossible to open. Smooth and solid. Impenetrable.

After a few minutes, I felt like it was real, and strong.

Ready?

I nodded.

I felt Nain's presence trying to make its way into my mind. It was almost physical. I could feel him inspecting the box, searching the sides, the corners, the top and bottom for signs of weakness. He started pushing at it, then harder. I focused on making the box stronger, holding it together. I felt sweat break out on my forehead, felt my box giving way under his power, and felt the full force of him in my mind.

He gasped and pulled back. I opened my eyes and looked at him.

"What did you see?"

"A young woman's body. Abandoned building."

I nodded. Made sense. Living nightmares and all that.

"Your mind is very strong. Your thoughts are clear. It almost feels like I'm living in them."

"Is that different than usual?"

"Yes. Usually, stored thoughts have a fuzzy quality to them. Things people are thinking or envisioning right that moment are crystal clear. The older the memory, the fuzzier they are."

"I haven't had much experience looking for old thoughts. I have only dealt with the immediate ones."

He nodded. "Again."

I rebuilt my shield, tried to make it stronger. We went through it all again. It took him longer this time, and I could hear his breathing escalate with effort, as mine did. He finally made it in, and I groaned in annoyance. He didn't leave right away, and I tried to push his presence out of my mind. He didn't budge.

Rage filled me. "Nain, get out," I said, opening my eyes.

He did. He met my eyes, and I saw the anger I was feeling from him reflected there.

"Jesus Christ. What did you see?"

"A basement. A man."

"Enough," I said, standing up. "This lesson is over. Fuck."

He stood up too. "I don't choose what to see."

"I know." It still didn't make it any less mortifying.

"Who was he?"

"A dead man," I said, heading toward the stairwell. Walked out of the loft and promised myself I wouldn't be coming back.

CHAPTER SIX

Of course, I went back. Between Nain calling and annoying/threatening me, and Brennan reasoning with me (something that annoyed me to no end) I finally agreed to go back. And, after a lengthy tirade about what would happen to Nain's nether regions if he didn't get out when I told him to, we got down to training again.

I'd managed to hold out for three days. The part of me that hated being told what to do, that just wanted to be left the hell alone, did its best to stay away. But the more reasonable part of my brain knew that if I wanted to learn how to control my powers, how to keep myself safe, I had to go back. I tried not to think about the whole demon thing….that was just too much. I practiced building my shield almost constantly, practiced holding it. It gave me a migraine every single time, but I felt like I was improving. It didn't take as long to build it now, and it felt, to me at least, a bit stronger than it did when Nain had first taught me how to shield.

So Nain and I ended up on the roof again, miserable summer sun beating down on us, and he worked at me. It took a lot longer each time, and I was feeling pretty smug. Finally, after several long minutes and both of us ending up breathless, he finally made it in.

"Out," I ordered. I felt Nain pull back, and I opened my eyes. He was watching me, and, as always, whatever I felt from him had a note of anger mixed in that set my teeth on edge. His knees were touching mine, and I tried not to think about it too much, about the fact that physical contact with him made me feel like I could do just about anything, that there was an elation I felt at the merest touch from him that made zero sense. I was also too stubborn to move away. Especially since it didn't seem to have any effect on him at all. Bastard.

"You've improved a lot, Molls. Damn, your mind is strong."

"What did you see?"

"You. You were a kid. And three boys were picking on you in an alley. You gave two of them bloody noses and kicked one in the balls, and they ran away." Humor rolled off of him, glinted in his eyes.

"Yeah. That was a good day," I said, laughing despite the headache that was coming on. "Are these ever going to stop?" I asked, rubbing my temples.

"They won't happen as quickly, once you get used to it. But with the amount of power you draw, it's likely that you'll always have them."

"Why?"

He looked as if he was thinking. "Our powers have a cost. The brain, even the supernatural or demonic brain, really wasn't meant to withstand the pressures telepaths put them through."

"My body hurts like hell when I self-heal," I said.

He nodded. "Right. There's always a cost. And even with our powers, there's only so much we can do. Learning our limits and knowing when we're in danger of pulling too much and getting tapped out is important. It's something you're going to have to watch out for, more than most of us."

"Am I really pulling that much more power?" I asked,

cocking my head to the side.

Nain nodded. "Brennan is the closest in power to you. He's crazy strong, compared to even most magic users. Both of his parents were powerful shifters. When he's around, I can feel a pulse, an energy signature that is undeniably him. It's there, and it's obvious, but it's not distracting."

I nodded. It was the same thing I felt around Brennan. "And me?"

"Being near you is like being locked in a windowless room with a tornado. Your power courses through you. It roars. It's suffocating."

I raised my eyebrow. That was similar to what I felt from him, but I thought he was being a bit of a drama queen about it. "Really? All the time?"

Nain nodded.

"It must be really irritating to be around me, then," I said, grinning in spite of how freaked out I was.

"For many reasons," he said wryly, and I shook my head. "Back to work."

Nain was still hammering at my mind when his phone rang.

"Okay. Break," he said, irritation flowing from him. "You were really doing well that time." Indeed. Sweat glistened on his forehead, and the neck of his t-shirt was soaked from the effort.

"Thanks." I hid a smile. It galled him to give me the compliment, and I knew it.

A few words from Nain's side of the conversation made it clear that something was up. He hung up and looked at me.

"Imps and lower demon disturbance in Hart Plaza," he said, standing up.

"Do you want me to come?"

His gaze flicked over me, and he glanced away again. "Do you want to?"

"Can I fight?" I asked, watching him.

"Like I could stop you if you wanted to," he said, irritated and amused at the same time.

"Then I'm in." We got in Nain's truck and drove the few blocks between the loft and Hart Plaza, on the riverfront. Storefronts and office buildings flanked the streets, their signs flashing and glowing, reflecting off of the hood of the truck as we drove. Nain was focused, not really in a talkative mood.

"So. The imps. What do I do?" I finally asked.

He glanced at me. "Kill them."

"Isn't that a little cruel?"

He glared at me, then jerked his eyes back to the road. "They're demonic servants, Molls. They're down there setting fires and hurting people, causing all kinds of mayhem. The more we dispose of now, the better. Evil little bastards."

"Like demons are evil," I muttered.

He let out an irritated huff. "This is not the time to have an existential crisis."

"Fine," I muttered waving my hand. I stared out the windshield.

He glanced at me again. "Any way you want to is fine. They're really not hard to kill. It's much harder to catch the little bastards in the first place."

I thought a minute. "So, are they just wild, unorganized pests? Or is there someone in charge?"

Irritation, discomfort rolled off of Nain. "They work for demons. High-level demons."

"Like you?"

He shook his head. "Worse than me." He was quiet a minute. "There are demons like me, that have some speck of humanity in them. Not much. Not enough to make a difference, really. But to demons, that little speck means everything. Nothing would follow a demon of my birthline."

"Except a bunch of magic-wielding freaks," I said, looking out the window.

"Yeah. Except for those. Imps and lower demons serve the strongest demons. They flock to those that have the most power. It's instinct, just the way they do things. And since most demons here are the typical, mindless destructive types…" he trailed off, shrugged. I got the picture.

"Are there many?"

He shook his head. "Most demons prefer the Nether. They can live there easily, without having to try to blend into a human society. But there's a whole lot of pain they can cause here in the mortal world, and that's like having crack sitting on a table next to an addict. Some can't turn away."

"So, this demon who gives the orders. Do you know who it is? Or where?"

Again, discomfort from Nain. "I know who it is. He moves around a lot."

I looked over at him. "Is there a reason we're not hunting his ass down? Wouldn't that take care of the imps?"

He rolled his eyes. "You don't just hunt down a high-level demon."

"So we just let him keep hurting people?"

Anger. "We bide our time, and we do things the smart way. We do what we can." He stopped the truck, jammed it into park, and turned to look at me. "Does that answer your question?"

I just looked at him and nodded. Anger still rolled off of him, felt like the tide coming in. I shoved my door open and got out.

As soon as I was out of the car, I could hear the sounds of chaos from the plaza. People yelling, screaming. A fight had broken out and was quickly getting out of hand.

"This is what they do," Nain said as we jogged toward the plaza. "They whisper in the ears of the weak, the ones most filled with rage. They give them an excuse to act out, they push them toward it. And it causes this, which causes pain, which makes their master all the stronger." His rage spiked, and his power rolled over me. I asked myself for the millionth time what the hell I was doing, and entered the fray.

Movement to my right caught my eye, and I looked. Imps, invisible to the eyes of the Normals, flooded the plaza. They were short, maybe three feet tall or so. Gray humanoid bodies, spindly arms and legs. Vaguely rodent-like faces with sharp teeth and beady black eyes. They surrounded the group of fighting people. Others climbed the sculptures, danced on top of the fountain.

"Like I said," Nain said, following my gaze, "do whatever it takes. Any that leave here will just show up somewhere else tomorrow, doing the same damn thing."

I nodded, and Nain ran into a crowd of imps, punching, kicking, tearing at limbs. The imps screamed and started to scatter. It would have been kind of funny if they weren't so grotesque. And if I wasn't still convinced that they deserved better than to be exterminated like roaches.

Sighing, I headed for another group of them before they could take off. I forced their will, made them stand right where they were. Then I forced each to strangle its neighbor. It was a brutal way to kill them, and it took longer than I would have liked, but it worked.

I felt like a monster. This. This was evil. Killing was not something I did. Ever. These were living beings.

Get the fuck over it, Molly. Nain's voice in my head.

I hate you.

No response. Once that group was dead (and disintegrated into nothing, handy, that) most of the imps were gone. I rushed several, punching and kicking the same way I saw Nain doing a few feet away.

"Molly," Nain shouted, pointing to the top of the fountain, where a few of the imps still danced.

He watched me. Waiting. A test. The imps stopped dancing when they saw me approach. There were eleven of them. They hopped down from the top of the fountain, and, as one, they bent a knee, bowed their heads, placed fists over where I guess their hearts were.

Did imps even have hearts?

I just stared at them. Felt Nain walk up and stand next to me.

"Well," he said. "I told you that you're powerful."

"What the hell does that mean?"

"They're swearing fealty to you. They're yours."

"I don't want them!" I yelled, then glanced at the imps, afraid I'd hurt their feelings. Did they have those? What the hell was I doing?

"They don't have feelings, Molly. They're primal. They follow power. They will do exactly as you say. Nothing more and nothing less."

"I don't want to be their master," I said, staring at him.

"Then kill them so we can move on," he said.

I clenched my fists.

"Do it, or I will. Decide," Nain said. I punched him in the stomach before I knew what I was doing, and was on him, trying to hit him again. He grabbed both of my wrists, held me at arm's length.

I used my knee, caught him not quite where I was hoping to. He wrestled me down to the ground and straddled me.

"Molly, stop it," he ordered. I felt my power building. I was pissed off, and I was scared, and everything I thought I was was wrong. Blasting him wouldn't solve it, but it sure the hell would make me feel a little better.

He groaned. "Would you dial it back, just a little," he growled. "You're pissed. I get it. Stop it."

My head was pounding. My body felt like it was about to split open from the pressure. Nain was angry, concerned, but not afraid.

"Why aren't you afraid of me?" I asked, and I heard the growl in my own voice.

"Because you're a good person. You may hate me, but

you'd hate yourself more if you ended me. We both know it."

"I can't kill them," I whispered, and hated the tears rolling out of the corners of my eyes. He still held me pinned to the ground while chaos erupted around us.

"Then lead them. Put them to work doing whatever it is you want them to do. More will come. Decide what you want to do, and do it. But you have to do something, Molls."

I nodded, felt my power receding a little, leaving a pounding head and an aching body.

"Get off me," I muttered, and he did, pulling me up with him as he did. The imps still knelt, and I left them that way. For now. Nain kept his hand on my arm as we surveyed the plaza. I pulled away, unable to deal with the way my demon, or my body, or whatever the hell it was, responded to his touch.

The fight between the Normals still raged on. Shouts, screams filled the night air, and I could see rocks and bottles being thrown.

"Time to do your thing," Nain said, nodding toward the crowd. "I'll watch your back."

I nodded, headed into the heart of the crowd. Rocks and bottles whizzed past my head. I was jostled, and one woman tried to hit me, but a look had her turning to find an easier victim.

I stood up on a bench and shouted. The crowd ignored me, kept fighting. I watched them go on pummeling each other, not even knowing why they were doing it, but totally invested in the fight nonetheless. I was still pissed, raw from whatever was happening with the imps. I could feel my power rise again in response to my anger. I shouted again. A few people, closest to me, turned and looked at me. The rest kept fighting.

"Hey, assholes," I roared, and the air seemed to vibrate, and everyone stopped moving and stared at me. I glanced at Nain. He was watching me intently.

"You are going to stop fighting." My voice thundered into the plaza. I felt the ground shake beneath me. "You are going to clean up your fucking mess. And you are going to peacefully go home and knock this shit off," I demanded. The night had gone silent around us, and the air crackled with my power. "It will be done." I focused, and with the words, the power fulfilled its duty. The people started milling around, picking up the garbage they'd been throwing, and slowly, mechanically, making their way from the plaza to cars and bus stops.

Once I was satisfied that I had them all under control, I jumped down and headed over to Nain. He was watching me, an unreadable expression on his face.

"What?" I asked, glaring up at him.

"You are one scary bitch," he said, and I felt just a twinge, a hint of pride coming from him.

"You say the sweetest things," I said, rolling my eyes. Then I glanced over at the imps. "To me, my imp-men," I said.

Nain laughed. "That was terrible."

I shrugged, and headed toward the truck. The imps followed. I seethed during the ride back to the loft. The imps rode in the bed of the truck, and stared at me through the back window the entire time.

"Are they going to spend all of their time staring at me?" I asked as Nain pulled the truck into his parking spot. He just shrugged.

We headed into the loft, and the gaggle of imps followed. "Imps, roof. Stay there," I said, feeling like an ass for ordering around beings that only came up to my thighs. They nodded, thumped their fists to their chests, and climbed the stairs that led to the roof.

When we got into the loft, Nain disappeared into his room. Brennan came out of his room. Ada and Stone waved me over to the dining room table where they were going over maps of the city, planning the team's next move.

"What's up with the big man?" Ada asked me.

"He's an asshole," I said, sitting down.

"Isn't he always?" Brennan asked, joining us.

Stone laughed. The three of them kept talking. George and Veronica sat in the living room watching TV., and I stared at Nain's bedroom door, willing him to come out. After a few minutes, he did.

Brennan glanced between us. "Uh, Molly. I'm going up to the roof for a while. Wanna come?" he asked.

I shook my head. "No thanks." He shrugged and headed up the stairway. "Just don't hurt the imps."

Brennan stopped still, turned, and came back down the stairs. "Imps? What the hell are imps doing here?"

"They're hers," Nain said, pointing at me.

"Oooooh," Ada said knowingly, winking at me.

"What?" I asked.

"That's why he's got a stick up his ass."

"I do not—" Nain started.

"Molly's stronger than Nain, Molly's stronger than Nain," Ada sang, laughing. Brennan joined her.

"I already knew she was stronger than me," Nain said quietly, and I could feel the irritation rolling off of him.

"Yeah, but now *everybody* knows it," Brennan said, still laughing.

"I need answers, Nain. Now," I said, standing up and walking over to him. "And I need them before I Hulk-smash you."

"Yeah? Try it, Molls," he said. His entire posture changed, ready to take me on.

"You knew that was going to happen," I said, feeling my anger spike. I felt raw, ripped open.

"I had a feeling," he admitted.

"And you didn't think to share that little tidbit with me?" I shouted.

"I wasn't sure. What the hell was I supposed to say? 'Hey, Molls, those little imps might decide to serve you, so be ready to have an imp army at your disposal'?"

"You could have said something. Could have warned me that this was even a possibility. What the fuck am I supposed to do with them?" I shouted, gesturing up toward the roof.

"Why do I have to give you all the answers? You're smart. Figure it out," he said, snarl in his voice.

And that did it. We started yelling at each other then, and I called him several choice names, and he kept drilling home how weak I was for someone so strong, and the more we shouted and argued, the higher our powers spiked, until it felt like the air around us was going to explode with it.

"I never even fucking wanted this," I shouted, and he was about to respond when Ada cut in.

"Hey, angry demons!"

We both looked at her.

"One: do you feel the building shaking? You want to bring down a few tons of rubble on us, because that's what you're about to do if you don't calm the hell down."

I forced my power down a little, felt Nain's draw down a bit as well.

"Second: both of you are doing that freaky-ass demonic glowing eyes thing, and it's gonna give me nightmares. Knock it off."

"My eyes are not…." I began, then I looked at Nain. His eyes glowed, orangey-red. "Oh, that is creepy," I murmured.

"Actually, I think it's kind of a hot look on you," Brennan said to me. "Nain, not so much."

I shook my head, felt the last of my power slither away from me. The next time I glanced at Nain, his eyes were normal, but still burning holes through me.

Ada laughed. "Thank you for not destroying our humble abode," she said. Then she looked at Nain. "Honey, it's been decades since I've seen your eyes do that."

He glanced over at her. "It's been decades since I've

dealt with anyone as infuriating as her," he said jerking his head toward me.

"You know what I think? I think you two should go somewhere, preferably an open area, maybe that empty lot across the street? And you should talk about this." Ada said. "Try not to level the neighborhood."

Nain walked out, and I followed. He stalked across the deserted street, and sat on what was left of the brick wall that used to surround the lot. I sat next to him. I could still feel irritation rolling off of him.

"I need answers. You're the only one who can give them to me. You know that," I said quietly. "I don't want to fight with you right now."

"Liar."

I shook my head. "All right. I do want to fight with you. But I need answers more than I need to fight."

"Fine."

"Can I trust them? If I have them help me, won't they just run back to their old master and tell him what we're doing?"

Nain shook his head. "They can't. Once they give their allegiance to a new master, they serve them, completely. It's not possible for them to double-cross you."

"Why not?"

"It's just not how they work. You've read fairy tales about beings that can't tell a lie if you catch them during the full moon, or give them something, or shit like that, right?"

I nodded.

"Okay. This is the real-life inspiration for stories like that. They can't lie, now that they've sworn to serve you. The moment they bent knee to you, they gave up the ability to serve any other."

"Until someone stronger comes along," I said.

"I don't think that's something you'll have to worry about."

I shook my head. "All right. So what can I have them

do?"

"Anything you want. Have them look for your lost girls. More eyes and ears out there. Have them get information for you. Have them scope out neighborhoods for us. Have them bring you a sandwich and give you a manicure. Whatever."

"Handy," I murmured.

"You could say that."

"So they can talk?"

He nodded. "They'll only talk to you, unless you command them to talk to another, or give them an order of some kind that involves talking."

I watched him. A muscle ticked in his jaw, the only visible indication that he was still pissed at me. I nudged him with my elbow. "So...can they live here with you?"

"Fuck no, Molly. Creepy little bastards."

"I had to try."

CHAPTER SEVEN

I ended up bringing the imps home with me. The dogs were less than thrilled with their new companions. I gave the imps the run of the basement, attic, and yard, and then I put them to work.

There was a little girl I was looking for. Kayla Martin. She'd been missing for almost two weeks, and everyone suspected her father. No one had seen him since Kayla had gone missing from in front of her house.

I sent the imps out, told them what I was looking for, and within hours they had a name. A friend of the girl's father, who worked at the same garage he did. I hung around, listened in on the man's thoughts. He knew where Kayla was. He was considering turning the father in. But he was afraid. He didn't want to get involved. I could see the house, clear as day, in his mind.

I sent the imps out again with a description of the house and general area, and they had an address for me within an hour.

A girl could get used to this.

I got ready. Dressed, filled the pockets of my cargo pants with things that I seemed to need less and less now that I was training with Brennan and Nain more often. My power was already higher than was comfortable; stress always did that. I gritted my teeth against it and tried to focus.

I looked at Kayla's photo from the newspaper. Beautiful little girl, a pawn in a fight over a nasty break-up. Soft, curly head of black hair, eyes like dark chocolate, dimpled smile, so full of joy it hurt me to look at her.

I patted Kayla's photo, went through the naming of the dead, my lost girls I'd found too late. By the time I was done, emotion, whatever had been, was gone, and I was cold. One thought: find my lost girl.

I jumped into the Barracuda, two of the imps in the backseat. I was going to see if they'd be useful as lookouts. I still didn't quite trust them, but I had to admit they were damn useful. I headed to the house I'd seen in the man's mind, the address the imps had given me. It was there, as he'd envisioned it, just off of Mack. Fire had destroyed the roof and parts of the second floor, but it was a brick house, and still appeared to be mostly solid. I walked up to it, tried to remember to breathe.

I listened as I got close to the house. Not a sound, other than the chirp of crickets, the distant sounds of traffic. I crept inside, one hand on my pepper spray, another on my flashlight. I glanced up and saw stars through the roof. She wouldn't be up there. I headed through, to what used to be a kitchen, long stripped of anything even remotely useful, right down to the copper piping behind the walls. I paused at the top of the basement stairs. If she was here, experience told me, this was where he was holding her. I went down, fully aware that if someone decided to follow me in, I could be dead before I knew what was happening. It was nothing new.

Down the rickety stairs, listening for any sound that might alert me to danger. The basement smelled of dampness, urine, feces. And something else, something worse. I looked through the small basement, saw nothing other than dirt, debris, stains on the floor that turned my stomach. I swallowed, forcing myself to keep my nerves down. It didn't work. My power spiked in response to my fear, the coppery smell of blood, to the knowledge that I had very likely failed this little girl. I felt rage creeping in, and I was soon almost delirious with it.

I headed back up the stairs. The lots around this house were like those in my neighborhood: overgrown and mostly empty except for decaying homes and dumped trash. I started looking, knowing, and dreading, what I would find.

It didn't take long. An area of flattened grass caught my eye, and when I wandered over to it, freshly turned earth. I stood there. Maybe it's a dog, I tried to tell myself. Maybe someone buried valuables there. Knew it was a lie.

One of the imps walked up and stood beside me. I couldn't tell them apart.

"We can dig, if Mistress wants," it said. I nodded.

They dug in silence for a few minutes, revealing what my gut already told me we'd find there. Her father had barely taken the time to dig deeply enough to bury Kayla securely. She was still dressed in the pink t-shirt she'd been wearing when she'd gone missing. A bullet to the chest had turned most of it brownish red. The imps turned, looked at me.

I knelt, put my face in my hands. Not praying. Begging forgiveness. I'd been too slow. I should have moved faster, started looking as soon as I'd found out about Kayla. Counted, ridiculous as it was, on a father's love preventing him from hurting his daughter. I bit my lip, hard, felt my power soar within me in response to my rage.

I looked at the girl again. So innocent. What had she gone though in the last days of her life? Tears stung my eyes. I'd never lost a child before. A baby. I'd lost too many grown women, a few teenagers. Seeing Kayla's tiny body destroyed me. She'd had her whole life ahead of her.

"I'm sorry, Kayla," I whispered, covering the body again, the imps helping. We had her nearly covered when one of the imps hissed "Mistress!" and I heard the grass crunch behind me.

"Stand up, real slow," a deep voice said. I took a breath, and stood. Cursed myself for getting so caught up that I dropped my defenses. "Turn around."

I did. The girl's father stood before me. I recognized him from the newspaper stories. He was short, stocky. Bald, with a neat goatee. Dressed in jeans and a polo shirt, as if he was getting ready to go meet the boys for a beer, instead of coming to check up on his dead daughter's grave. The daughter he'd murdered. I could see it there in his mind, over and over again. Anger and fear rolled off of him, and it turned my remaining sadness to rage, fed my demon in a way that nothing else could.

"You shouldn't have come here."

"Was it worth it? Did killing that baby solve all of your problems?"

He didn't answer me, but the gun started to shake as his hand started trembling. The way he stared at me, the terror rolling off of him, made me wonder if my eyes were doing the freaky demon glowy thing again. A moment listening to his thoughts confirmed it, and I smiled at him, baring my teeth. It wasn't meant to be comforting.

He lifted the gun higher, aiming for my head.

I didn't hesitate. Attacked his mind, ordered him to drop the gun. There was no persuasion, no willing. I just forced my way in and made him do what I wanted.

God, it felt good.

I could feel my power gathering around me, knew that if I didn't control myself, I would destroy him.

He still held the gun, still pointed it at me, though he was screaming now, words unintelligible in his fear. The acrid smell of sweat, the scent of urine, stained the air, his terror permeating the night.

More.

I forced myself all the way into his mind, and he shrieked in agony. The sound sent chills down my spine. I felt my power grow, and watched him kill his daughter, bury her, feeling nothing but hatred for her mother. Nothing for his own flesh and blood.

I felt the moment I lost control. I ripped, like a wild animal, some kind of vicious predator. Slowly but surely drove him insane, until there was nothing left, until he lost the will and ability to live. His shrieks died as he did, and he fell to the ground, twitching as the life left his body.

My power snapped out. Too much. I closed my eyes. My head was pounding, and I could feel blood pouring from my nose. I knelt down and retched. I couldn't move. There wasn't an ounce of strength left in me, and all I could do was look over at Kayla's father's body.

Murderer.

I was a murderer.

I drifted out of consciousness, only coming to when I heard footsteps crunching in the dry grass behind me. Felt worry, and a warm hand on my back. The imps were back, crouching in front of me.

"Oh my God," Brennan said behind me.

"What the hell are you doing here?" I asked weakly, my voice muffled by the tall grass. I didn't have the strength to pick my head up.

"I felt you. You were pulling enough power to level a small city. Jesus, Molly." He sat down next to me. "The imps led me the rest of the way."

"She was just a baby," I said, my face still buried in the grass.

"I know," he murmured, sadness from him, worry. He was still and steady beside me, and I appreciated the calm.

"I was too late." I felt my head spinning. I forced myself up and looked at Brennan. He put an arm around my back, helped me sit up the rest of the way. I closed my eyes, and his arm tightened around me. We sat that way for a while, in silence.

"You're in no shape to drive," he finally said, his voice soft, seemingly aware of how my head pounded. "Let me drive you home."

I nodded, and Brennan held a hand out to me and pulled me up. The trip home was a blur, and the last thing I saw was Brennan closing my bedroom door behind him on the way out.

When I woke up, I was somewhere soft. I opened my eyes slightly, then closed them again. It hurt too much to open them. I lay there for a few more minutes. Everything hurt. I took stock. My body ached as if I'd gone ten rounds with Muhammad Ali and didn't have the power to self-heal. My head pounded, and I felt like I had thrown up everything, including a few internal organs.

I could feel power in my house. More than just me. Brennan's pulsing energy. Ada's steady hum. Stone. Ah, crap.

Nain was there, too.

I groaned and pulled the covers back over my head. Worked at maintaining my mental shield. It only made the headache worse, but I didn't need Nain in my mind right now.

Murderer.

The thought came, unbidden and definitely unwanted. Me, the real me, the me that was more about saving people than destroying them….that "me" was sickened, depressed, horrified at what I'd done.

But my demon, the part of me that I was having a really hard time claiming or accepting, was thrilled. Satisfied.

How did Nain live like this?

Remembering that he was there, I knew I had to get up. Nain would not leave until he'd made his point. Loudly. I grimaced and tossed the covers back and swung my legs off the side of the bed. I was still in the clothes I'd been wearing the night before, but someone had removed my shoes.

I got up and made my way to the dresser to grab some clean clothes, then across the hall to the little bathroom.

The overhead light made my head hurt so much the room spun. I closed my eyes for a few seconds, then opened them. I looked in the mirror. I was pale, even for me. And my eyes were dark, the normal gray more of a gunmetal. I frowned at my reflection. My face was clean. I distinctly remembered bleeding all over myself.

I slowly washed and got dressed in a pair of jeans and a black top. I brushed my hair and clipped it loosely at the back of my head. Then I went into my office and clicked on the desk lamp. Looked at the bulletin boards.

I gently removed Kayla's photo from the "lost" board and tacked it up onto the third board. The one I hated. "I'm sorry," I whispered, forcing myself to look at Kayla's face.

I would have stayed there, replaying all of my faults, every single thing I could have done differently, but I could feel Nain's power roaring from nearby, maybe the back yard. He wouldn't leave until we'd had this out. I steeled myself and made my way downstairs. I could hear the television on in the living room. It sounded like "I Love Lucy" reruns, the laugh track echoing up the stairway. I started down the stairs, and saw that Brennan was sitting on the bottom step, arms resting on his knees, watching TV.

"Why are you sitting there?" I asked as I crept down behind him. He turned his head and glanced at me.

"Nain's on the warpath. I didn't want him to bother you until you rested more," he said, turning back to the television. I sat on the step above his, studied his back, his shoulders. His hair just brushed the top of the collar of the flannel shirt he was wearing.

"What time did he show up?"

"Around six."

"What time is it now?

"Little after eleven."

"Please tell me you haven't been sitting on the stairs for five hours."

"Okay."

We sat in silence for a minute. I glanced toward the living room. Veronica, Ada, and Stone were all sitting in there. Veronica caught my eye and gave me a tiny wave. I gave what was probably a sickly smile in return.

"How are you feeling?" Brennan finally asked, still facing toward the living room.

"Like shit," I said.

He nodded. I didn't get him at all. I could feel trepidation, concern, from the others. I wondered if they knew exactly what had happened. But from him, nothing ever but warmth. He knew exactly what I'd done. And of the whole group, I'd come to see Brennan as the most altruistic, the most just genuinely *good*. Yeah, he was terrifying in his way. But you just knew, with Brennan, that he'd use every bit of his power to do the right thing. He should be horrified, sickened by me.

I knew I was.

He turned and looked at me, met my eyes. "You've never killed before."

I paused. "Not like that."

"You're going to explain that later. But for now, know this: it was him or you."

"I can self-heal," I reminded him. "I could have been more gentle. Part of me wanted him dead." I pulled at a thread on my sleeve, unable to look at him anymore.

"Of course. Part of me is glad he's dead. It doesn't make us evil, Molly."

I shook my head. "I shouldn't have done it, though. And definitely not like that."

At that moment, I heard the back door open, felt Nain's presence in the house before I saw him. He walked into the living room, looked up to where I was sitting.

Oh, he was *pissed*.

He glanced toward the living room, at the rest of the team sitting there. "All right. You've all seen her. She's alive and moving. Time to go."

Ada and Veronica got up, headed for the front door. Stone gave me a quick smile, then walked outside.

"Call me later, Molly, okay?" Veronica said as she headed outside. I just nodded. Nain turned back to me.

"You too, Brennan," he said, eyes on me as he said it. I tried to calm down. My stomach churned. All I wanted to do at that second was run.

"Nain, man, maybe you should go home for a while. Cool down a bit," Brennan said, not moving, standing between me and Nain.

Nain was about to say something, when I put a hand on Brennan's shoulder. "It's okay, Brennan," I said.

I felt irritation from him, but he nodded, got up. He met my eyes for a second, then headed out after the rest of the team.

And then it was just me. And one very, very pissed off demon.

CHAPTER EIGHT

Nain and I watched each other. When the last car had left the driveway, I felt my stomach plummet.

The bastards had actually left me with a demon who was clearly ready to do some damage.

Team mates, my ass.

He stood there, three hundred pounds of rage, watching me. Crossed his arms over his chest. Even if I couldn't feel it coming from him, I'd have to be blind not to know how angry he was. His eyes had been glowing fiery orange since he'd entered the room, and a muscle ticked in his jaw.

"You've put me in a very fucked up position, Molly," he finally said, voice low, deadly.

I watched him. Readied my body for fight or flight, whichever would work better.

"Now I need to decide what to do about you," he said. "Do I keep you around, because you're powerful, and deadly, and we need someone like you?" He paused, sapphire gaze boring into mine. "Or, do I put you down like the rabid dog you're likely becoming? Try to save the world from the shitstorm I knew you'd be?"

I felt my demon rise in response to the threat. Power

surged through my body. "You could try that. But from what I can feel, it wouldn't go well for you." I ignored my wobbly legs, less wobbly already. My power was feeding me, strengthening me. The imps had left wherever they'd been hiding, gathered on the stairs around me. One, the one I'd come to think of as the leader, snarled.

Nain's power rose in response to mine. My house started trembling, like a mini earthquake was hitting my neighborhood. The floors upstairs squeaked, and I heard glasses clinking together from the kitchen cabinets.

"You're strong. But I'm experienced. I would not have any problem taking you out. Bending you, breaking you. And you know it," he said, walking toward me.

I knew it. I could fight, but he could still kick my ass. I could try to level him with my power, but he knew how to finesse power in a way that still escaped me. I could try to shatter his mind, like I'd done with Kayla's father, but he was still stronger mentally than I was.

I tamped my demon down, took a deep breath. "I didn't mean to do it, Nain," I said.

His power only heightened. "All of this time, we've been working on control. He was a fucking Normal. That level of power was totally unnecessary." He was shouting now, voice thundering through the house as it shook around us.

"I know," I said softly, trying to soothe. "I know. I let myself get too emotional. I lost control. It was unacceptable."

He drew back, just a little, enough so I could breathe. He cocked his head to the side, still watching me. "But it felt good, didn't it?"

He knew. Of course he did. I nodded. "It felt amazing."

He closed his eyes, took a deep breath, and I watched as he worked at getting himself under control.

"For someone who keeps preaching control at me, you sure seem close to losing yours a lot," I said. He opened his eyes and glared at me.

I really should learn to think before I speak.

He was nose-to-nose with me in an instant. "And it's just lucky for you that I'm not as weak as you are, isn't it?"

I backed away. He followed. I tried ducking under his arm, and he blocked me. I shoved him (which was like shoving a concrete wall) and he grabbed my upper arms, and his power spiked again.

"Don't you get it? I do not want to destroy you, Molly," he growled. And I felt something from him, something that scared me more than his rage.

It must have shown on my face. He released me, stepped back and raked a hand through his hair.

Then he laughed. "Is that what it takes to really scare you?"

I didn't answer.

"Don't worry. I don't want you. My demon does. Do not confuse the two."

"You are a demon," I said weakly.

"As are you. Demon wants demon." He shrugged. "It doesn't mean anything. We are not animals."

I stood there for a minute, looking anywhere but at him. I started talking, words tumbling out of my mouth, hoping to fill the awkward silence. "I didn't know how to stop it. I went in, and I was ripping him apart before I even realized it was happening. By the time I had it together enough to stop, it was too late."

Nain nodded. "Like you said, it feels amazing to destroy. I can't destroy mentally the way you can. That's…..well. That's something different. It's easy to lose yourself in the lust of destruction."

"I don't want to use my powers anymore," I said, my voice barely a whisper.

"Don't fear them. Control them."

We stood in silence again, me a few steps up the stairway, Nain at the base of the stairs. I leaned on the wall, rested my aching head against the cool plaster.

"If you had to kill me, could you? Really?" I asked.

He glared at me, then turned and stalked into the kitchen.

I followed him. He was standing at the kitchen counter, leaning on his hands. "I need to know."

Nain looked at me, met my eyes. Silent.

"Can you? If you have to do it? If I get out of control, can I count on you to end me? Because I don't want to be a monster. I felt what I can become, and it is terrifying. And you know it. You've known it since before we talked that first time."

"I am powerful enough to destroy you," he finally said.

"But will you? If I become that, can you swear to me that you'll kill me?"

He didn't answer.

"Please," I heard the desperation in my voice, and hated it. I felt tears threatening, fought them back.

"How about this?" he finally asked. "We work on making your control so complete that there is no danger of you losing yourself?"

"I will work on it. But I still need you to promise me."

I met his eyes. His jaw clenched. Frustration. A terse nod, and I felt a little bit of the weight lift off of my shoulders.

If I'd thought that training with Nain was an exercise in misery before, it was worse now that he'd devoted himself to "Operation: Control." When I wasn't working, and I wasn't out prowling the streets and looking for lost girls, I was with Nain.

I was getting rather sick of him.

"Again," he commanded. We were sparring on the roof of the loft. It was easily nearing a hundred degrees, heat shimmering off of the roof around us. While Brennan taught me a more martial arts style of fighting, Nain's style was closer to how I normally fought — street fighting, i.e., use what you've got, fight dirty if you have to.

So we fought. And every time one of us (usually me) lost, we'd just start again. But it wasn't just physical fighting. We fought mentally at the same time. I maintained my mental shield, kept him out of my mind, and kept my temper and my demon in control while I worked at not getting my ass kicked by him.

It was exhausting.

He was brutal. In every way. Six feet, six inches and three hundred pounds of what seemed like nothing but muscle versus all five foot four, one hundred thirty-ish pounds of me. He did not let up on punches or kicks the way I knew Brennan did when he felt me tiring. He hammered at my psyche, threw insults at me verbally and mentally. He exploited every weakness he knew I had, until every nerve was raw, every emotion I'd ever had was magnified by about a thousand-fold. And here we were, doing it again.

He got me down, pinned me again, making it clear I was immobilized and very much defeated, and I shoved at him. Nain got up and walked over to the table, started guzzling a bottle of water. Sweat soaked his gray t-shirt. I glared at him as I grabbed my own water bottle.

"Any reason we're not doing this in the nice, air-conditioned loft?" I asked, pulling my own shirt away from my sticky body.

"Aw, is the little princess sweaty? Poor baby," he said, taking another drink of water.

I gave him the finger. And he ignored it.

"How often do you fight in nice, air-conditioned places?" he asked.

I didn't answer. Knew he was right.

"I hate you. You know this, right?" I said as I walked across the roof to where the chaise lounges were. My body was healing itself, and I needed to sit. My head pounded, but I was getting used to the pain. Where it had been debilitating before, it was merely an annoyance after the last couple of weeks with Nain.

I closed my eyes and let my body do its thing. It burned, like always. Muscles repaired themselves, fractures (yeah, I had them, always, after going a few rounds with Mr. Congeniality) knitted together, fresh skin regenerated, leaving scrapes, cuts, and bruises nothing more than a memory. I could feel my body shifting, flowing, the sensation not unlike being pulled apart from the inside out.

I felt Nain walk past me and settle into the chaise lounge near mine. He was quiet for a few seconds. "Your control's getting a lot better, Molls," he said.

"I still hate you."

He laughed. "Do you think that bothers me?"

"No. But it makes me feel better to say it."

I felt a small spike of irritation from him, and I smiled, eyes still closed against the blazing sun.

"You do that on purpose," he said, annoyed.

"What?" All innocence.

"Try to get a rise out of me and then gloat when you manage to."

"Payback is a bitch."

Nain went silent and broody. We sat there for a while. He was still irritated. He was tired, and in pain. I forgot sometimes that, demon or not, he didn't have a healing factor like I did. And I might be lacking in the verticality department, and the muscle department, and the experience department, but I pack a mean punch thanks to my power. I gave as good as I got.

Well….almost.

I glanced over at him. His arm was over his eyes, shielding them from the sun. His other hand rested on his stomach. Knuckles bruised, scraped up, from fighting me. Swollen lip, black eye, again, from me. And probably many bruises on his chest and stomach from me, too.

The bastard had earned every one of them.

"Like I was saying. Your control is getting really good," he said.

I didn't answer.

"Don't you think it's time to start using your powers again?"

I answered him with silence, felt his irritation spike.

"You've kept a lid on it, Molls. You've worked really hard. I've done everything in my power to enrage you, and you've kept a tight rein on your demon. We need you."

"It was still you, though. I wouldn't kill you," I mumbled.

"Why not? I thought I was pretty much first on your shit list." I heard the smile in Nain's voice, more than saw it. Felt satisfaction from him.

"Don't get too pleased with yourself," I muttered. "You are. But I still don't want to kill you."

"Aww. She really does care," he said, tone laced with sarcasm. I glared over at him, shot a blast of energy at his chaise lounge, sending both him and the chair crashing to the roof deck.

Nain laughed as he picked himself up. "There she is. The bitch is back."

"I'm not using them out there. No."

He shoved me over, sat on the edge of my chaise lounge. "Molly. I'm not fucking around here. We need you. I've given you space. I know you need to do your thing. I know you need to work through this, but we're running out of time. We're exhausted."

I looked up at him. I knew the team had been fighting on too many fronts. Werewolf pack on the southwest side, weirdo coven of witches in the northern part of the city. But they were exhausting themselves now fighting against a pyro that was causing trouble on the east side, torching neighborhoods, just generally causing panic. The official word from the Detroit P.D. was that there was an arsonist on the loose. Which I guess was technically correct, except that this one didn't need gasoline and matches.

The team had been fighting him for a week now. He had a crew of witches and a few lesser demons working with him. Nain and the crew had taken out the strongest of his demon buddies, but he was still wreaking havoc. I'd barely seen the rest of the team; they were usually passed out in their rooms when I arrived after work. Nain was even more tired than the rest; when he wasn't fighting, he was training me.

"He's tearing these neighborhoods apart. He's forcing people out of their homes. People are dying, Molly. We don't have the luxury of letting you extend this particular pity party for yourself."

"I'm not ready," I said. "What if I lose control again?"

"If you do, we'll work on it more. We'll keep working on it. But we need you to do this now. We can keep him busy, fighting out front. You do your thing from behind the scenes. Convince him to stop. Bend him to your will, make him behave. We've tried everything." He paused, and I could feel frustration flowing from him like a tidal wave. "It's impossible to fight someone when all they have to do is blast a fireball at you."

I sighed. "Yeah. Okay." I could stop it. They deserved a break. I tried to ignore the dread settling in the pit of my stomach.

Nain reached up, tucked a stray curl behind my ear, gently ran his fingertips through the strands. I stopped breathing. His deep blue eyes met mine.

"You're afraid again," he said softly. "I've spent two weeks hurting you, in dozens of ways, in every way I'll let myself hurt you, and I don't see real fear in your eyes until now." His gaze burned into mine, and he leaned forward, just slightly. I felt a tremor run through my body, felt my heart race as he closed in. His lips were a hair's breadth from touching mine, when I felt someone nearby, and pulled away.

Within seconds, the roof door opened. Brennan walked out and glanced between me and Nain. I felt irritation, disappointment from him. My face was burning, my heart still racing.

"Brennan?" Nain growled, backing away and standing up. Relief. I could breathe again.

"Veronica and George are fighting again. He's moving out. He says he's done, with her and the team. I did everything I could to talk some sense into him, and so did Ada and Stone." He shook his head, "They're ridiculous. I think you need to deal with it," Brennan said.

Nain nodded and stalked through the door without another word. Brennan stood there, watching me.

"Training, huh?" he said, raising an eyebrow and walking over to the short wall that surrounded the roof.

"Yeah."

I walked over to where he was, leaned against the wall next to him. "I'm going to be going with you guys to fight the pyro tonight," I said.

He nudged me with his elbow. "Are you ready for this?"

I shrugged. "I don't have much of a choice at this point. I can't keep letting you guys get the shit kicked out of you when I could stop it."

"Superior, much?"

I shrugged. "It's the truth."

He let out a short, bitter laugh. "You've been spending too much time with Nain."

"Yes." We sat and watched the sun set over the city, waiting to find out where the pyro would pop up that night. The tiny bit of a cool breeze was a welcome change from the sweltering heat earlier in the day. We sat side by side on the wall, feet dangling over the side of the building. Mostly silent. Brennan was one of those people you could just relax with. We didn't need to talk. And I wasn't much for conversation anyway. Every second that passed brought me closer to having to use my powers again, to using them on someone's mind. I knew…if I hurt the pyro, it would be something he deserved. It didn't make it any better.

And the worst part of it is that part of me, the dark

part, the part Nain and I had been trying to put into a cage, was looking forward to it.

The roof door opened and Brennan and I both looked that way. Ada stepped out onto the roof. She looked at us, gave one slow nod, then gestured toward the door.

CHAPTER NINE

"Guess break time's over, huh?" Brennan asked her as we followed her.

"Sure is. He's over near Livernois, not too far from the U of D campus," she said.

We stepped off the stairway to see the entire team getting ready. Stone shrugged on his leather jacket, his own version of armor. Veronica gave me a wave, went back to the meditation she did before these missions, eyes closed, lips moving in some type of silent mantra. George paced. Nain stood at the windows, looking out. To say that everyone was tense didn't do it justice. This was a group of pissed off, exhausted people. Volatile. The power and emotions swirling in the room made me nauseous.

I was re-braiding my hair, mostly for something to do. Nain turned, glanced at me, then looked away. "Okay, people," he said. "This will hopefully be the last time we fight this fucker." A small cheer went up from the team, glances thrown my way, and I tried to look confident.

"We're going to go in like we always do. Do what you do, as if nothing is different. We need to distract him so Molly can work at him," he continued.

"Won't he feel her?" George asked, looking at me, as

always, like I was some kind of venomous snake. I was tempted to hiss at him.

"He will. It's impossible not to feel her nearby," Brennan said.

Nain nodded. "Which is why we have to do a good job trying to distract him. We do our job right, he won't know she's nearby until it's too late."

Ada was standing next to me. She reached over and gently took my hand, gave it a squeeze. I gave her a small smile and squeezed her hand in return.

"The most important thing is that we give Molly what she needs," Nain said, glancing at me again. "How much time will you need?"

I shrugged. "No idea. I've never tried this on anyone with power before."

"We're so screwed," George groaned. Veronica glared at him and Stone smacked him in the back of the head.

"Shut up, son," Stone muttered.

"If she can't manage it, we'll fight, just like we always do," Nain said. He looked at me again. "But I don't think it's going to go down that way."

Stone pulled on his leather gloves. "Let's do this, then."

We squished into Nain's truck. Me between Nain and Brennan in the front seat, Ada, George, and Veronica in the extended cab. Stone followed us on his Harley.

The tension in the truck was insane. Nain and Brennan talked to each other a little on the way, mostly about where to hit them, where to position the team. The more I was with the team, the more I saw the inner dynamics. Nain was clearly the leader. Brennan was his second in command, the one the team members seemed to feel most comfortable dealing with directly. Which was fine with Nain, who generally didn't say much to anyone unless he was giving orders. Ada and Stone were next in the chain of command, with George and Veronica at the bottom of the totem pole.

Me? I wasn't part of the team. No pecking order for

me, thanks.

We got to the neighborhood where Ada's informant had reported the pyro, and I could smell the smoke. The sky was orange.

"Molls. We're going to face him. Find a good spot and do your thing," Nain said as he put the truck in park.

"You're having her go alone?" Brennan asked.

Nain snorted. "Anyone dumb enough to fuck with her is going to regret it the second she starts putting the hurt on, trust me."

Irritation from Brennan.

Nain continued. "We'll keep him busy." He met my eyes. His voice in my mind. *You can do this. You're a demon. This guy is nothing compared to you.*

I nodded.

No fear.

I nodded again.

"Man, I hate it when you two do the creepy telepath thing," George muttered. Brennan laughed, and everyone opened their doors. We took off in different directions to do our thing.

I ran around, heading for the streets beyond where the pyro was. There weren't as many vacant homes in this area, not like in other parts of the city. I crept through back yards. I could hear the screams, smell the smoke, from where the pyro was. I ended up climbing into some kid's old tree house, the wood slightly rotten from years out in the Michigan weather. I could see the chaos.

A tall man stood at the center. Ebony skin, wearing a summery white shirt and khakis, leather sandals on his feet. He looked like someone ready for a walk on the beach. But he raised his hands, and a nearby garage exploded in a ball of flame. More screams.

Nain and the crew were doing what they could. Nain and Brennan (in his panther form) charged him. His goons kept them busy. Ada was focused on keeping a protective mist over the area. Normals would not see most of what was happening — how the hell would we ever explain it? Veronica and Stone fought some of the other goons, and George was slipping into the shadows, trying to sneak up on the pyro. They were keeping the focus well away from me.

I focused on the pyro. Emptied my mind of anything but him. I started poking at his mind, the way Nain did to me when we were training.

It wasn't even hard to find a way in. This was a seriously messed up individual.

I traveled the pathways of his mind. I could sense his rage, his sense of superiority. His lust for destruction. Guy would have made a spectacular demon.

He felt me. I knew it the second he did. Panic. An immediate attempt to shut his mind, but I was already there, and, new as I was at this, I was stronger than he was.

"Who is doing that?" he screeched into the night, looking around, swiveling from one direction to another. I continued working at his mind. I could feel, practically see, very clearly, where his power was. I tried reasoning with him first.

"You hate fire. Fire is your enemy. You fear it. You will surrender now. It will be done," I said in his mind.

Confusion. And then he laughed, and threw a fireball at Nain and Brennan. They both dove out of the way in time, but he shot another one.

I gave up reasoning. I saw his power, tried to disconnect it from him, tried to choke it off. He screeched, laughed, slapped at his head as if I was an annoying mosquito or something.

And he threw more fire. I heard Stone roar in pain, saw Veronica get thrown at least twenty feet by the blast of a fireball hitting a nearby house. Kids were crying.

My heart was pounding. I could feel panic creeping in. What if I couldn't do it?

I kept working at figuring out how to cut him off from his power. I tried distracting him, commanding him. He was insane, and nothing was working. The more scared he got, the more fire he threw. Garages, homes, sheds were going up in flames, more and more the longer I messed around. He'd stopped focusing on the team, in full panic mode now, and in his panic, more destruction.

I was starting to get desperate. I jumped down out of the tree house, walked toward where he was. He turned and saw me. Exactly what I wanted.

He watched me, and I felt fear, anger course through him. He readied a fireball.

And I focused. I couldn't cut him off from his power. I couldn't reason with crazy. I acted on pure instinct.

I focused on his power. It was there, bright and throbbing in his mind. And I hungered for it. I wanted it. I had already invaded his mind, seen his memories, lived his life alongside him. Now, my attention was focused on that warm, perfect, nourishing power.

It should not have been possible to do what I did next.

I devoured it. I ripped his power from his psyche without any mercy, without any gentleness. It was mine. This was not mere destruction. This was destroying, then pillaging, his strength being absorbed into my body.

Oh, it was good.

His screams sent shivers up my spine, and his power filled me. I kept walking toward him. He looked at me one last time, and fell over, nothing but an empty skin.

The night was deadly silent. And then all of his people went crazy, started fighting our people. They were terrified. A few started to come toward me, and Nain crashed into them, flattening them, then going to work with his fists. Within seconds, they were still. Knocked out. Without their leader, they didn't pose much of a threat anymore.

Some of the pyro's people had Stone cornered. He was hurt badly. They were doing that pack thing, going after the weakest one.

"Hey, assholes," I said, and my voice thundered

through the neighborhood. I could sense the team watching me. The pyro's people turned to look at me, too. I could feel their fear, and it filled me.

I smiled.

And snapped my fingers.

And a fireball appeared in my hand.

Screams, running. But they couldn't run fast enough.

Their pain was so good. Their fear fed me, completely. I readied another one. Felt their panic grow, and relished every bit of it. They tried to run.

"Molly," Nain said, standing in front of me, hands up, out, a gesture of peace. "You got them. You did it." He met my eyes.

The fire rested in my palm, practically begging me to throw it. My heart raced, and I hungered for more.

More fear.

More pain.

"Molly. Look at me. Stop it," Nain said, a growl in his voice. Fires raged behind him, flames licking orange and blue along the homes damaged by the pyro, the bodies set aflame by me.

"Don't threaten me," I said, and my voice was barely my own.

"No threats. Time to stop now, baby." His eyes held mine. Glowing orange. *Don't make me do this. Not now.*

My head was swimming with my lust for destruction, adrenaline from watching my friends battle for their lives, hunger for more fear, more pain.

I bit my lip, forced my demon down, reluctantly. The fire went out.

I collapsed.

And blessed blackness followed.

I came to in the truck, slumped against Nain's arm while he drove. Brennan was on the other side of me, Ada and Stone in the back seat. I kept my eyes closed. Facing them right now was not something I could do.

I knew it was wrong. Whatever I'd done back there, whatever I'd done to the pyro. It was wrong. I took his power. I could still feel it, thrumming inside me alongside my own. How long would I have it?

Was I a thief in addition to being a murderer?

It was quiet. I could feel tension, fear from Nain's team.

"Are you going to talk to her about this?" Ada finally asked, quietly, from the back seat.

Silence for a few seconds. I started to think Nain wouldn't answer. "What am I supposed to say to her? 'Try not to kill any of us, please?'"

I felt irritation spike from Brennan. "You're not going to say that."

Silence. Then: "I should."

"You need to tell her she's still got a place with us," Brennan said. Something in the way he said it made my heart melt, just a little. "You need to tell her she's still got friends."

"You need to tell her what she is, big man. She needs to hear it from you, before she hears it from somebody else," Ada said. "Whatever you decide to do, you know I'm with you. I always have been. But she needs to be told, Nain."

"Stone?" Nain said. I waited.

"She saved my life, man. That's all that matters to me right now. Call me a selfish bastard if you want to, but I like the chick."

Ada laughed a little. The mood in the truck lightened, just a little. Except for Nain.

I shifted, forced my eyes open. I looked straight ahead. Couldn't make myself meet anyone's eyes.

Ada reached forward and rubbed my shoulder gently. "You did good, girl."

I snorted. "I'm a goddamned monster."

I could sense a little fear from Ada. Concern, anger from Brennan. Nain was a mess of emotions I couldn't even begin to sort out.

"Maybe, baby girl," Stone said from the back seat, his voice hoarse from the pain. "But you're our goddamned monster."

Ada laughed and gave me another pat on the shoulder. Nain pulled up in front of the loft. "Everyone else out. Go get some sleep. Molly, you're with me."

I didn't argue. Brennan glared at Nain, glanced at me, but left just the same. Stone and Ada walked into the loft, supporting each other. I scooted over into the passenger seat Brennan had vacated, and Nain pulled away from the curb.

I tried to glance at him without being obvious. He was a coiled spring. Jaw clenched, every muscle in his arms and shoulders tense. Blood flecked his neck, and his shirt was torn. His hands gripped the steering wheel so hard I was surprised it didn't snap. I turned and looked out the window.

He drove across the Belle Isle bridge, taking us onto the island. This time of night, on a weeknight, it was mostly empty. He drove around to the beach side and pulled over.

We sat there for a minute, listening to the engine tick as it cooled down.

"I need some air," he finally said, shoving his door open. He walked toward the beach, and I followed. There was a bench nearby, and he sat on it, staring out at the Detroit River. I sat at the other end of the bench and looked over at him.

Blood was seeping from his shoulder.

"Oh, holy shit. You're bleeding," I said. He waved me off, but I headed back to the truck and grabbed the first aid kit from under the front seat. I ran back with it, walked up to him.

That side of his shirt, the side I hadn't been able to see

when he'd been driving, was soaked in blood.

"That needs to be cleaned and you should go to a hospital or something," I said, stepping back.

"It's just a scratch," he muttered.

I stepped closer to him, sat on the bench on his injured side. I gently pulled the fabric away from his shoulder. It was already sticking to the blood there.

"Oh, crap," I said under my breath.

"It's not that bad. You don't have to do anything. I'll take care of it later," he said. Fury, a million other emotions.

"It's just gross, that's all," I said, pulling the tattered shirt back again. I went to work with the alcohol wipes, cleaning so I could see what I was working with. A long, ragged gash went from his shoulder to just below his neck.

"That's not from a knife," I murmured.

"Broken bottle," he said, clenching his jaw as I applied more alcohol. My stomach turned as blood continued to ooze from the cut.

"I am really bad with blood," I said, putting a gauze pad over it.

He didn't say anything, and I kept working, securing the gauze with tape. This close, I could smell him, and he smelled like cinnamon, something warm and almost spicy. Even in my fear, my stress, I found my mind going to earlier that day, that near-kiss on the roof. My fingers ran along the tape, sealing the gauze to his cool skin.

"Do you know what you did tonight?" he asked quietly.

"Yeah. I took his power."

"There's a word for that. Mindflaying."

"Okay."

"Demons can't do that. At least, I didn't think they could. The last being I heard of who could do that was well before my time."

I was silent.

"It's–" He sighed. "It's not good, Molly."

"I'm a demon. There is nothing good about me," I

said, pulling his bloody shirt over the bandages. I started repacking the first aid kit.

"Mindflayers are feared by our kind. Mindflayers are the boogeymen that supernatural kids fear. Even demons fear the mindflayer."

I just watched him.

"You're like the psychic equivalent of a vampire, Molly. You don't need blood. You feed on power. You can feed on thoughts, emotions." He paused, looked out at the river, at lights reflecting on the water. A few seconds later, he continued. "When I found out you were able to read emotions, I suspected. But then, I thought it was not possible. Yet here we are."

"You're a danger to the supernaturals, whose power you will find more and more irresistible. Your hunger will only grow, now that you've had a taste. And you're a danger to the Normals, who are nothing if not emotional. Temptation is everywhere, for a mindflayer."

He wasn't looking at me.

"They won't feel safe around me anymore," I said softly, thinking of the team. George, who already feared and hated me. Veronica, who wanted to be friends, but jumped every time I glanced her way.

He was quiet. "Some of them won't. Some, like Stone and Brennan, will. But the question is, do you want to risk it?"

"I would never hurt one of you," I said.

"You might not be able to stop yourself."

"Do it, then."

He looked at me, finally, deep blue eyes that always seemed to see straight through me.

"End me. Do it now. I won't even put up a fight." Knew it was a lie as the words left my mouth. I practically felt my demon salivate at the thought of a fight. And he knew it, too.

He laughed. "You would. Once your demon realized what was happening, you'd fight. And given what you are, you might even win, if you got lucky."

"So, what? You're afraid of me now?" I asked, exasperated.

"Did I fucking say that?" he asked, glaring at me, and his anger fed me.

Fed me.

Why hadn't I realized it before? Being around Nain, I always felt stronger, faster, more powerful.

"Oh, crap."

He was watching me, and I sensed satisfaction from him. "Anger is good, huh?"

I nodded.

He stood up, and walked toward the water. Raked his fingers through his hair.

"We had a deal. You would at least try to end me if I became a monster. This pretty much defines 'monster,' doesn't it?"

"We'll keep working on control."

I got up and stalked over to where he stood. "Did you see what I did tonight?" I asked, well aware that I was shouting. "I killed him, and I liked it. I killed his team, and I liked that. I didn't want to stop!"

He turned to me. "Yeah. I saw it. It was magnificent."

"I....what?"

"Keep working, Molly. You're too tough to let it win."

"But you just said it's only going to get worse."

"Yeah. But you just proved something for me."

"What?"

"You can feed pretty well from me. Hell knows we're a mess together. When aren't we pissed off at each other? Training, working with the team, you'll be around me enough to take the edge off, I think."

"You think? I don't want to....feed from you," I said, wrinkling my nose.

"It will work. I'm a demon. I'm full of rage. You want rage. You'll want more of it. Match made in hell." Then he snorted. "It's not like I'm asking you to bite my neck or anything."

I blushed. And he laughed, and I sensed hunger from him, need. "Unless you want to."

"Oh, Christ," I said, stalking back to the truck.

He laughed behind me, and I gave him the finger without looking over my shoulder.

I didn't know whether to be relieved or upset that he hadn't killed me.

After my little demonstration with the pyro, and the subsequent talk with Nain, things between the team and I were just awkward. No matter what Nain said about my ability to control it, I knew now what I was. And now that I knew, it explained some things.

Being at work, or out in crowded places, had always set me on edge in a way that went beyond annoying. While some people joked or fantasized about causing serious damage to their co-workers, I could actually do it. It was temptation at its finest. The fact that my co-workers were complete morons just made it all the more tempting.

It was maddening. Work and social situations always had been, but I just thought it was because I was an antisocial bitch. Of course it was that, but so much more. It was slow torture.

It was like going a whole day with a freshly baked, fragrant apple pie sitting right there in front of you, and not being allowed to have a bite. It was like staring at a tall glass of ice water after running a marathon through hell.

I was starving.

Nain had been right. Now that I'd had a taste of power, now that I'd been fully and completely fed, it was almost impossible to focus on anything other than having more. There were emotions to feed on: annoyance, irritation. The daily dramas of the Normals I worked with barely took the edge off. Worthless.

And I was, of course, avoiding everyone I knew who

was *not* a Normal.

I'd been ignoring calls from Nain and the rest of his team for over a week. I was still ashamed about what they'd seen me do, despite their kind words and the effort they'd made not to seem terrified of me. And then there was their leader. The idea of "feeding" from Nain in any way was so screwed up I didn't want to examine it too closely. I knew logically why and how it worked. It didn't make it any less embarrassing.

Starving.

I sat in my cubicle staring at the clock at the bottom of my monitor and willing it to speed up. I had finished all of my work by ten o'clock, just like every other day. My co-workers were all chatting each other up. They tended to avoid me, for the most part.

I can't imagine why.

I heard the outer office door open, sensed Brennan before he said a word.

"Hey. Is Molly around?" he asked our receptionist. I rolled my eyes at the thoughts that went through her mind as she looked him over. Idiot.

I took a deep breath and walked out to the reception area. "Hey."

Brennan stood there, leaning on the front counter. Dressed, as always, in a pair of well-worn jeans and a white t-shirt. I'd asked him once why white, and he'd said it was easy to bleach the blood out of it.

How practical.

He smiled when he saw me, a real smile accompanied by a genuine sense of happiness to see me. Concern, but happiness.

"Hey, beautiful. You about done here?"

I felt heat rise to my face as the receptionist and another coworker watched me with renewed interest. And more than a little jealousy. I smiled back.

"Ten more minutes. Want to hang out while I finish up here?"

He nodded and followed me back to my cubicle.

I sat down in my chair, and he sat in the only other chair, after removing a pile of files from it.

"So. Why are you here?" I asked quietly, knowing there would be ears straining to hear what the creepy data entry clerk had to say to the male model who'd come to visit.

"You weren't answering any of my phone calls or texts," he said, just as quietly.

"I haven't been answering anyone's calls or texts."

"Yeah, I know. You owe me for keeping Nain off your ass, by the way."

I laughed. "I bet. Thanks."

He just nodded.

"So, what? Is there a work thing I'm needed for?" I turned my monitor off and set my phone to voicemail.

"There's always asskicking that needs to be done. You know that. But it can wait for tomorrow. You feel like grabbing something to eat?"

I almost choked.

"I think that's probably a really stupid idea. No offense," I added quickly.

He laughed. "None taken. Shockingly enough, I'm not afraid of the big bad mindflayer."

I glanced up, met his eyes. Blue. What was it with blue-eyed men in my life all of a sudden? Not Nain's sapphire blue. A slatey, blue gray that made me think of a lake during a storm. "Maybe you should be," I muttered.

"Am I tempting you?" he asked, cocky smile firmly in place.

I glared at him, stood up and grabbed my messenger bag. He followed me out of the office as I made a point of not telling my coworkers to have a nice weekend.

"Come on, Molly. You choose. I'll even pay."

I rolled my eyes. We walked through campus. "Are you trying to kill me?" I asked. My chest, my body, burned with hunger.

"Nope. Trying to prove a point," he said.

I glanced at him.

"You can do this." He said it, and he was so confident I almost believed.

"And if I can't? If I end up taking all of your lovely shapechanger powers from you and leave you an empty husk, or, even worse, dead? What then?"

He reached out, took my hand, dragged me closer to him. "I trust you."

I pulled my hand back and moved away. "You're an idiot."

He grinned. I felt warmth from him, straight down to my toes. The crazy son of a bitch genuinely liked and trusted me. Me! I shook my head.

"Are you gonna make me beg?" he asked, still smiling.

I rolled my eyes. "Fine. Just...stay away. Not so close." He took a deliberate step away from me and grinned again. This was a phenomenally stupid idea.

We ended up at Supino's in Eastern Market. We sat side by side scarfing slices of the perfectly crisp, gooey pizza as we looked out the window at the market. I devoured my pizza, hoping it would keep me distracted from Brennan and his power. Every time my mind strayed to the power I could feel radiating from him, I forced it back to the pizza, or what was happening outside. Anything but how tempting it was to take a trip into his mind and take what I wanted.

His knee was pressed against mine under the counter. Not his fault — the restaurant was packed and everyone was smashed together. I turned to look at him. "I need to ask you something."

"Sure."

"That night with the pyro," I said, dropping my voice. He nodded, leaned in. "There were demons there."

He nodded again.

"Real demons. They actually looked like demons." I remembered them: built like very squat, muscular men. Skin the color of dried blood, some with skin the gray of clayey soil, absorbing all of the light around them. Orange glowing eyes, terrifying faces, sharp horns and teeth. Claws.

He nodded again.

"What's the deal with Nain? Why doesn't he look like that?"

Brennan winced. "Oooh. That's a sore spot."

"Tell me," I said, taking another bite of pizza.

Brennan sighed. "You can't tell him I told you." I nodded my assent, impatient. "He used to look like that, when he wanted to. He wore his human skin most of the time, but when he needed to kick some ass, he dropped the enchantment. I remember him looking like that when I was little. Scared the shit out of me, to be honest."

I watched him. "I didn't know you've known Nain that long."

"My parents were part of Nain's crew. They died when I was nine. Nain raised me," he said quietly.

My jaw dropped. Brennan looked at me and laughed.

"I'm sorry. About your parents, I mean."

He shrugged. "It was a long time ago. They died with honor, doing the right thing. And, though you probably won't believe me, I had a good childhood."

I raised my eyebrow and he laughed. "Really. I did."

"If you say so. I want to hear more about Daddy Warbucks later. Back to the demons."

He smiled. "Something happened. He never really told me what, but he lost his demonic form. I don't know if it was a fight or a deal, or witchcraft, or what...but he lost it. And when he lost it, he lost a good portion of his power." He met my eyes. "He's powerful now. He was a freaking nightmare when he had access to his natural form."

"So, whatever happened to him, it stuck him in a mortal body," I said.

He nodded. "Weaker. He could do all kinds of crazy shit in his demonic form. He hates it that it's gone. He had to learn how to be a badass in a skin."

"He pulls it off," I muttered.

"Yeah."

We were quiet for a minute. I plucked a few stray mushrooms off of my plate and popped them into my mouth. "I never had one to begin with," I said.

"Yeah. You're not all demon, though."

I stopped. "What do you mean?"

"You're not. You and Nain feel similar, but not the same. You didn't know?"

I shrugged. "I just assumed. I had no idea I was even a demon until Nain told me. Besides, what non-demon would mate with a demon?"

"Sometimes there's no choice," he said carefully. My stomach turned. "And sometimes, there is, and beings want one another in spite of what they are." His gaze met mine. "Whatever you are, Molly, you're not just a demon or mindflayer. There's something else there, and it's noble, and fearless. That's why I'm not afraid of you. I believe in you."

"I don't," I said, looking out the window.

"You should," he said. We were quiet for a few minutes. Then: "I answered a question. Now it's your turn."

"I didn't agree to answering anything," I said, still looking out the window.

"It's only fair."

"Fine."

"How'd you get started finding lost girls?"

I took a breath. "I never knew my parents. I spent my childhood getting moved from foster home to foster home. More frequently the older I got." I looked at him. "I was a pretty creepy kid, I guess. I didn't know to hide what I could see. It freaked several of my foster families out."

"I bet."

"But I made it through, and I figured out that I wasn't crazy, just telepathic. That saved me from a few messed up situations, actually." I paused, drank some of my Coke. My junior year in high school, my foster parents were real creepers. I'd asked to be moved, but the agency was dragging its feet, and I was tired of the game. I was working at a little diner, and the manager was nice to me. Helped me out, listened to me. I trusted him."

"I ran away from home, and the manager told me he had a spare room and I could stay with him until I got on my feet. I was stupid enough to take him up on it."

Brennan took my hand, held it in his lap. I continued. "He was nice at first. And then one day, I woke up in the basement, duct taped to a chair."

I felt, more than heard, the growl emanating from Brennan's chest.

"He never touched me," I said. "It was all mind games. He spent every second when he was at home threatening me, telling me how weak I was, how worthless I was, that I'd never become anything, that I'd never be free. It doesn't sound as bad as what he could have done. And it probably wasn't. But months on end of hearing it, over and over again, the constant threat that he just might decide to do more, and feeling helpless to fight either way….it seriously messed with my head. And add to that that I could hear every thought he was having, feel every emotion he felt…" I shook my head. "There were days, during and after, when I was sure I was losing my mind. When I was scared of every shadow, every sound."

Brennan seemed to be holding his breath. "No one came for you?"

I shrugged. "No one cared enough to look. My foster parents never reported me missing. The state is overburdened as it is. They lost track of me. No one knew I was gone."

I looked down at our hands clasped together. Foreign, this being connected, in any way, to another person. I frowned.

"How did you get out?"

"That was when I really realized what I could do. When I started being able to force my will on others. He was there, doing his normal shit. And I just kept thinking stop, shut up, just stop it over and over again. And suddenly he did. And I thought he was messing with me, more mind games. So I told him to release me. And he did."

"And you ran?"

I didn't answer.

"Molly?'

I closed my eyes. "Remember when you asked me if I'd ever killed before? And I said 'not this way?'"

Dread from Brennan. "Yeah."

"I told him to get gasoline. Told him where to pour it. Told him to sit, stay. And told him to light himself on fire. And I walked away as it all burned."

We sat, and his thumb stroked the back of my hand. "A lost girl," he said softly.

I nodded. "After I was free for a while, I started getting my head straight. And I decided that there were too many of us out there, girls no one would bother to find, girls failed by everyone around them. I could help them. So I started."

We were quiet. "I didn't know it then, and I'm not even sure now, but I think he was a demon. In a skin, but a demon just the same. He felt like one. I just didn't know demons existed back then."

We sat in silence for a couple of minutes, his thumb still stroking the back of my hand. "Ready to get out of here?"

I nodded. Brennan got up, pulled me with him, and we left the restaurant.

"Why aren't you disgusted?" I asked him finally. We were strolling through the streets, back toward the parking lot, my hand still clasped in his.

Brennan looked over at me. "Because if you hadn't

done it, I'd be hunting his ass down right now. Am I supposed to hate you for avenging months of mental and emotional torture? Am I supposed to be disgusted because a confused teenage girl snapped and lashed out at the one being who deserved it? Human or demon, whatever he was was a monster. Monsters deserve to die."

I swallowed. He was still looking at me, heat in his gaze.

"I know Nain preaches control at you so often that you see any loss of it as a failure on your part. But I'm a shifter. We have a different outlook on these things. Sometimes, death is necessary. Revenge is noble. Kill, be killed. That's the only choice given to us, sometimes."

He started walking again, pulled me along with him.

"Does Nain know you feel that way?" I asked.

He winked. "Why do you think we don't get along all that well? He needs that control. It's made his life possible. No one in the supernatural community would trust a demon to keep them safe, otherwise. He is control. It's practically his religion."

"It works for him," I said, aware again of how much I craved the power coursing through Brennan's body.

He glanced at me. "Yeah. But some things just can't be controlled. And that's when instinct takes over."

CHAPTER TEN

I spent the weekend finding lost girls. Now that I had the imps at my disposal, I was finding more of them than ever before. The media circus that had become "the Angel" was only growing, and I was starting to realize I had to make a choice soon: embrace the attention, hoping it would make anyone thinking of hurting a girl in my city think again, or start forcing my will on those I rescued, so they couldn't remember me.

Even thinking of doing that to girls and women who had already suffered made me hate myself a little more.

It was Sunday afternoon, and I was beat. I'd been out all night Friday (after my dinner with Brennan, which I was trying not to think about too much) finding lost girls, grabbed a couple of hours of sleep on Saturday and went out again. Later that night, I'd do it again.

I was mowing the lawn around my house with my little old-fashioned reel mower while the dogs patrolled the property and the imps watched from the roof of the house. They seemed intrigued by the mower. Must have been all those blades.

I tried not to think too much about the imps, either.

I had already ignored four calls from Nain. Brennan

had been (thankfully) giving me space. I figured he knew I needed it after socializing on Friday. Socializing is more tiring than fighting demons and other supernaturals, hands down.

So I had an afternoon to myself before going out again that night. I had a lead on two more lost girls that I wanted to follow up on. But, for the moment, it was just me, my house, my dogs, and a couple dozen imps.

Of course, that was until I saw Veronica's little blue Ford Focus come racing down the street toward my house. I sighed. What the hell was wrong with these people? My throat burned. I fed a little from the thugs I'd saved my lost girl from the previous night, but it was hardly enough.

They didn't have real power. Not like Veronica.

I closed my eyes, took a deep breath, and forced my hunger down. I'd have to do something about it soon.

Later.

I opened my eyes, and Veronica was getting out of her car.

"Hey!" she said, smiling. I could sense nervousness from her.

"Hey. What are you doing here?"

She laughed. "You don't have to act so happy to see me," she said, sitting down on the porch steps.

I stood there, crossed my arms, tried to ignore the burning in my throat.

"You look just like Nain when you do that," she said, laughing again.

"And now she insults me," I muttered, pushing the mower toward the side of the house. The imps jumped down and started inspecting it. I glanced at Veronica, who was watching the imps with an expression of fascinated horror on her face.

"So. Welcome to the loony bin. Why are you here?"

She rolled her eyes. "Reasons. First: message from Nain. And I quote: 'Start answering your fucking phone or I'm coming over there no matter what Brennan says about giving you space."' I rolled my eyes. "And second: I needed to get away for a while. George has been a real son of a bitch since I broke up with him, and it's only gotten worse since the whole mindflaying thing," she finished.

"He still wants to quit?" I sat down on the lawn, away from her.

She nodded. "Brennan talked him out of it twice already. Really, George has nowhere to go, but he hates pretty much everyone on the team right now."

We were quiet for a few minutes. "Why did you break up with him?" I finally asked.

"He's been pushy lately. He hit me, and that was the last straw."

I looked at her. "He did?"

She must have heard the threat in my voice. She smiled. "I handled it. One thing about having my specific set of powers: no one can physically hurt me without getting hurt much worse. He hit me, and he went to hit me again. When his hand landed on me the second time, he got a little taste of what I can do. He was paralyzed for about twenty minutes."

I looked away. My chest tightened, and it took everything in me to ignore that voice in my head urging me to take her powers. Useful. Deadly. They'd be so good to have…

I shook my head. "So you came to hang out with me."

"Well, you're so much fun, you know."

"Yeah."

She laughed. "And I was hoping I could go with you if you're finding your lost girls tonight."

I stared at her. "No."

"Oh, come on. It'll be fun."

"Yeah, right. As long as I don't lose control somehow in the heat of the moment, and as long as everything goes just right, and as long as you have the sense to stay away from me."

"See? What could go wrong?"

"You people with your 'I believe in you' shit are going to get yourselves killed," I muttered.

Veronica didn't answer, but I did sense a tremor of fear from her. And it was good.

"You need to work on your control. I'm your friend, or I'd like to be. I'm willing to be scared of you, to put myself in danger because I believe in you. You kind of owe it to me to at least try," she said.

"What kind of moron puts themselves in danger like that?" I scoffed.

Her eyes met mine. "The same kind of moron who goes out alone rescuing lost girls from god knows what."

I shook my head. These people. "Fine. You can back out at any time, otherwise don't cry to me if you end up having to kiss your powers goodbye. We're looking for one lost girl tonight: Dorothea Hopkins. I know where her boyfriend is going to be later. I'm pretty sure he's the one that has her. If I can pick up a location from him, we'll be doing a rescue tonight."

Veronica grinned. "Excellent."

Veronica and I had cereal for dinner, because it was all I had in the house and it seemed rude not to offer her something. I tried, several times, to tell her not to come with me, that it was a stupid idea. I came this close to forcing my will on her. I could have. I probably should have. She would hate me, Nain would lecture me until I was ninety, but at least I knew she'd be safe from me. She laughed me off.

I ate two huge bowls of Cookie Crisp, trying to abate some of my hunger. It was a distraction for as long as it took me to finish the cereal.

I ended up leaving Veronica in the kitchen while I went upstairs to get ready. "This is so stupid," I muttered to myself as I pulled on a black t-shirt. Two of the imps, the ones I'd started to think of as the leader and his/her (I couldn't tell the difference yet between male and female imps, or if there even was a gender difference) second in command, were sitting on the rocking chair in my room. I'd gotten used to them being around, for the most part. I glanced at them. I'd given them orders, but other than nods and chest-thumping, they'd never responded to me.

"You can talk, right?" I asked as I started filling my pockets.

"Yes, mistress," the leader said in a gravelly voice. I nodded.

"You know what's going on with me. The mindflaying thing."

They both nodded.

"How do I stop it?"

The leader looked at me, consternation on his homely little face. "You don't. You take. You kill. Is the only way to satisfy the need."

"Anger fills me. I can feed from anger, right?"

He/she nodded. "It will not be as satisfying. Mistress would do better to take what she needs. Make her strong."

I glanced at him once more, and he nodded, ears twitching. "I can't."

"Then mistress will grow weak. And mistress's enemies will win."

"Who? The street thugs?"

He/she gave me a withering glare. "Worse. Puppeteer. And he who pulls Puppeteer's strings."

"I haven't heard from her since that night," I said. "She's scared of me."

"Scared of Mistress, yes. But she craves Mistress's powers. Mistress is a powerful weapon."

"I'm nobody's weapon."

"No?" The imp scratched his bony knee. "What about demon skin?"

"Nain?"

He nodded, once.

I was silent. Turned to the mirror and pulled my hair into a low knot. "I'm not his weapon, either." The statement was met with silence. "So who pulls the

Puppeteer's strings, then?"

Silence.

I turned back to the imp leader. His mouth was clamped shut.

"Tell me."

He didn't answer, shook his head.

I was starting to get angry (easy, since I was always on edge lately). "I command you to tell me," I said.

The imp only shook his/her head more furiously. I recalled something Nain had told me.

"You can't, can you?"

The imp nodded.

"Former master, huh?"

The imp nodded again.

"Nothing? Not a name? A clue? A hint?"

The imp opened its mouth, tried to say something, and its voice died in its throat. It shook its head apologetically.

I bit back my frustration. "It's okay. Not your fault." I sat on the bed to put my shoes on. "Do something for me," I said quietly. The imp leader and its helper leaned in toward me. "I'm going to slip out the window. Hopefully, by the time she realizes I'm not here, it'll be too late. Do not, under any circumstances, tell her what you know about where I'm going tonight." I could hardly contain my hunger anymore. It filled me, felt like being pricked with rusty needles from the inside out. I couldn't do this. I couldn't risk it. But I could put all of this energy to use saving a lost girl.

"Promise me," I whispered.

"Promise, Mistress," the leader said, and he thumped his fist once on his chest. His assistant mimicked his gesture. I nodded once. I was done with this. I was cutting myself off from the group. I couldn't do it anymore, and they refused to listen to me.

Getting out of the house was easy. I slipped out my bedroom window, down the roof, and climbed down the trellis next to the front porch.

The car was the bigger issue. My Barracuda was loud. It was a muscle car, after all.

So, public transportation would have to do. I jogged for the nearest bus stop. This was such a pain in the ass.

After finally catching a bus (freaking DDoT, man) and two bus transfers, I made it to the location the imps had given me. The house was there, and so was the boyfriend's car, just as the imps had described it. I crept around the house, keeping close to the foundation, trying to hear anything happening inside. A back window was open, and, the closer I got, the better I could distinguish several deep voices.

Most of the conversation was focused on the card game going on and the music on the radio. But the thoughts I picked up gave me a good idea of what I was looking for.

An apartment, a quad. Not too far from here. I fixed the imagery in my mind. She was there, chained to a rod in the closet, bound, gagged, starving. But alive.

So much anger, fear, hopelessness. What could make one person hurt another so badly? I listened more, got a better read on where the woman was being held, and got ready to leave.

"How's Thea doing?" one of the men asked. I stayed put, after all.

I could sense irritation from the room. Boyfriend. "She threatened to leave me again. She's having a time out until she comes to her senses."

There were a few seconds of silence. No one was surprised, I realized. One of the men thought, *again with this shit?* I shook my head.

"You better hope that bitch that finds the lost girls doesn't end up on your ass," one of the guys at the table said.

He was met with a grunt.

"That bitch is spooky. Creeps up on dudes, pow! They

don't know what hit them, end up shitting their shorts and shit."

"Those stories are bullshit, man. You hear the description of her? Tiny bitch, barely five feet tall? Doesn't even use a gun? Explain that shit." There was a grumble of general agreement from the four guys around the table.

The conversation moved on to something else, and I slipped away. Luckily, the house he had stashed Dorothea in was only a few blocks away. I knew where it was a surely as Dorothea's boyfriend did. Sometimes, telepathy is damn convenient.

I jogged the few blocks to the quad, cutting through backyards when I was able to, and just generally trying not to be seen. About fifteen minutes later, I was there. The house was in decent shape, but the shrubs around the porch were overgrown, and the lawn was straggly and long.

My lost girl was in one of the two upstairs apartments. This was an old-fashioned quad, with stairs running up the back of the house to the two upper flats. I went up the stairs silently, listened at one window, heard a TV and a baby inside. I listened at the other. Silence

I'd hoped he'd left a window open, but I wasn't that lucky. I took my lock-picking set (which I'd barely used — stuff like this was not my strong suit) out of my pocket and worked at the lock, listening. The last thing I needed was for someone to sneak up on me now. I looked around. This was all creepier than it should have been. I wondered again if I should have let the imps come with me. I wasn't overly fond of them, but at least it was someone who could watch my back.

Damn, I was hungry. I tried to ignore it. Tried to focus on what I was doing. The latch clicked, and I turned the knob, then shut and locked the door behind me.

The apartment was sparsely furnished. A couch and a TV in the living room, a card table and chairs in the kitchen. The bedroom was down the hall, along with a bathroom. I pulled a small penlight out of my pocket and made my way to the closet. I opened the door, and the young woman, Dorothea, looked up at me, wincing from the bright light.

I pointed the light at the floor.

"It's okay. I'm going to get you out."

Dorothea started sobbing, and I worked at the padlock on her chain. It had just clicked, when I heard the front doorknob start rattling.

"Fuck," I muttered, Dorothea sobbed. I shushed her. I put my hands in my pockets. Readied my pepper spray and knife.

Footsteps came toward the bedroom, and I stood at the ready, barely breathing. The bedroom door opened.

"Honey, I'm home," the man from the other house said. And he switched on the light.

"Welcome home, darling," I said. The man jumped, then reached into his waistband.

"You don't want to do that," I said, lacing my voice with will. He looked uncertain. Then he shook his head and continued to pull the gun. "I'm giving you one last chance. Drop the gun. Step away. And then don't fucking move. It will be done." My power snapped, and his eyes went blank. The gun fell from his hands, and he looked at me, confused.

I walked toward him and kicked the gun out into the hallway, reached into my pockets for zip ties.

"Guns. Weapons for cowards," I growled, leaning in to tie his wrists together. He was deathly still. A blank look remained in his eyes. I looked at him.

Something was not right.

His eyes were completely blank, his face slack after that initial confused expression. He didn't move. I went into his mind, tentatively.

There was nothing there. As if he was empty. No. Broken.

He was broken. I'd bashed my will into his mind with

so much force I'd destroyed him. There was nothing there. The man was a vegetable.

I stared at him. I'd done this. In my rage, my hunger, I'd lost control with yet another Normal. A piece of shit Normal, yes, but a Normal just the same.

I remembered Dorothea, then. I walked, in a daze, to the closet and finished freeing her. The woman ran over to her captor.

"What did you do to him?" Fear. Of me. Something in me woke up, savored that fear.

I shrugged.

"You did something to him! He'll be okay, right?" Dorothea's fear reached a fever pitch, and I soaked it in. So good.

"Are you kidding? He's been beating your ass and keeping you locked in a closet," I said. "He didn't care about you nearly as much."

"He loves me," Dorothea insisted. "He just can't control his emotions."

I looked at her. "Are you telling me you would have preferred to stay in the closet?"

Doretha shook her head. She looked at me. Her fear hit me then, full on.

Her eyes. Why-the-hell-are-her-eyes-glowing-like-that?!

I savored her fear for a minute, as she sat, terrified, next to her vegetable of a boyfriend.

And then I went into her mind.

I removed every memory of myself.

And I locked the door behind me when I walked out.

I stormed down the back stairs, fuming. Headed toward the nearest bus stop, trying to figure out what the hell I'd just done. Completely drowned in guilt, anger. So when I'd wandered a few blocks, to a less-populated part of the neighborhood, and looked up to see the street blocked by two cars and a half dozen or so heavily armed men, it was too late. Guns were pointed solidly at my head, and I had nowhere to run.

The men watched me. They were all big, burly men. Dressed alike. Same posture, same expressions. I stopped walking a few feet from the cars, running through options in my head.

"Angel," the man closest to me said. "Our Lady has a proposition for you."

"What is it?" Sizing him up, weighing my options.

"Our boss wants to give you another chance. Come with us, quietly, and you won't get hurt."

"And your boss is?"

"The Puppeteer."

"Ah. Of course. That explains some things. Does she make you all dress the same or was that by choice?"

The six of them looked at each other.

"Our Lady likes us to present a certain look," the leader finally said.

"You look like a boy band. Except that one doesn't match. His shirt is cut totally wrong," I said, pointing at one of the guys at the rear of the group. They all turned to look at the offending sextuplet and I took the opportunity to bolt back into the neighborhood.

I liked to fight. There was a time to fight. This was a time to run my ass off and hope I was fast enough.

I heard guns firing, felt bullets whizzing past me like angry hornets. There were shouts behind me.

I ran through the neighborhood, jumped a few fences, zigzagged through a few streets. I lost a few, but there were two behind me. They must have split up, trying to box me in.

I put on a burst of speed, ducked into a garage. I left the old-fashioned garage door swinging slightly open. Held a canister of my pepper spray in each hand.

And the two puppets came around the side of the garage. They opened the door, and they each got a full-force, point blank dose of pepper spray. They went down, shouting in agony, and I jumped over them and ran back the way I'd come, zigzagging through yards, hoping the misdirection would throw off the other puppets.

I was just thinking I'd managed it, when I saw three more. They'd spotted me, and were running toward me, guns firing. I took a bullet to the thigh (again. Damn!) but I was determined to keep running. They followed, and my leg slowed me down while I healed myself.

They were catching up with me. Running was not going to work. All they had to do was get one or two more shots in, and I was screwed. Time to switch tactics. I stopped, looked at them. "You hate guns," I began, power filling my voice. One of them laughed.

"Your powers are shit compared to the ones our Lady has."

"If you'd have come with us, we would have been forced to keep you safe."

"But since you ran, we get to do what we want."

"And take you to our Lady anyway."

The way they switched off, almost completing each other's sentences, should have been creepy. But I was full of adrenaline and power, and I burst out laughing. I felt my power building.

"You want me? Come on then, big boys."

They approached me, warily, guns drawn and pointed at me.

"We're going to rip your body to shreds."

"All we have to do is keep you alive."

"But you'll wish you were dead."

I crossed my arms, shook my head. I hoped I looked cooler than I was feeling. My heart was about to pound out of my chest, and I felt like I was going to puke. But my power was filling me, near to bursting. I had to trust that it would be enough to keep me safe now.

They came closer, maybe four feet away now.

"She's so scared she can't even move."

"Not so tough now."

"I get first dibs."

I closed my eyes, pictured going inside the triplets'

minds. It was agonizing. One on one was one thing, but that was not possible. The Puppeteer had a hook into them, mentally, and they were linked together.

Which explained why they talked in such a damn creepy way.

I couldn't just change their minds. The Puppeteer was strong. They had been so fully tampered with, so fully wired to obey her orders, that there was no changing.

I couldn't even read their thoughts. My head started pounding as I made my way into their minds. I was there. I could see the Puppeteer's connection to them as if it was a physical thing.

I felt one of them grab me and pull my arms behind my back. I forced the panic away, kept working even as another shoved at my clothing.

I kept at their minds. The power and fear filled me, completely. Hands were on my body. All the hot showers in the world would not be enough to make me feel clean again.

I pushed away the fear. Focus.

I used my power, my anger, my fear, and I started attacking their connection to the Puppeteer. There was nothing for me to take here. It was a matter of complete destruction.

Leave nothing.

They started screaming.

I kept ripping.

And something snapped. I opened my eyes.

The one that had been on holding my hands behind my back fell, hard. The other two, who had been pawing me, fell to the ground, marionettes without their strings. I tried to sense for them. Nothing.

My head pounded. My nose was bleeding, and my body hurt all over between being shot, healing, and then being manhandled by the triplets.

I slowly stood up, pulled the ripped remnants of my top into some semblance of order. I pulled the knife out of my pocket and tucked it into my sleeve, out of sight but at the ready.

My powers wouldn't save me if another baddie came my way. It had taken an incredible amount of power to destroy the triplets. I was tapped out. At that moment, I probably couldn't read a thought if it was being mentally shouted at me.

Gone.

I walked toward where I thought the nearest main street, a street with a bus stop, might be, well aware that I was stumbling like I was drunk.

Of course, there was that last puppet that I hadn't dealt with yet. And just my luck that he'd seen me before I saw him. He walked toward me, grinning.

"I am so sick of you ugly motherfuckers," I muttered. My head felt like someone was hitting it with a hammer, and they just hit harder every time I spoke.

He came toward me. I hoped the knife would be enough. I ached, and I was exhausted. Powerless. My body was healing itself from the wounds I'd taken, but that requires energy. The energy that my body was putting into healing was more than I could spare if I expected to fight this last one.

"Too weak to fight. Perfect," he said. "This is why she made me the leader. The others were stupid enough to face you in a fight."

I just glared at him. Gritted my teeth. Trying to look like I wasn't on the verge of pissing myself.

"You look like they roughed you up, though. Did you manage to kill them before they enjoyed themselves too much?" And he laughed. "Nothing left to fight me, though."

Cocky son of a bitch.

He gave me a shove, and I fell to my knees. He kept walking toward me. "Let's get you trussed up so I can deliver you to my Lady," he said. "Be nice, now," he said, grabbing my hair and pulling a syringe out of his pocket.

He was in close. Which was exactly where I needed him to be.

I struggled to free my hair from his hands, keeping his focus on taunting me, and I pulled the knife out of my sleeve.

And slashed up, stabbing him in the thigh. I'd been stabbed there before. Bleeding out from a femoral carotid would be a quick way to die. He screamed in pain and rage. Doubled over on himself, screaming. And I took the opportunity to smash his head into the concrete, knocking him out.

"I think your idea of 'nice' is different from mine," I muttered, standing up and stumbling away.

I stumbled as far as I could, ended up falling against a tree. Nothing left.

It was just that kind of night. I was about to pass out. I wasn't even positive where I was, exactly, in terms of the nearest main street. And who knew when or if more Puppets would come after this group?

I pulled my phone out of my pocket. Prayed, for once, that Nain would answer.

He answered on the first ring. I almost cried in relief. "Hey. It's me."

"Molly. What's wrong? I swore I felt something…" he said.

"Yeah. I need you to come and get me. I just got my ass kicked, and I'm tapped out," I said, fighting back tears of frustration, fear, pain, embarrassment.

"I'll be there. Where are you?"

I told him where I was, as best I could. I could feel myself losing consciousness.

"I'll be there, Molly. Stay on the phone with me." His voice faded a little as he said "Brennan, let's go."

I heard him moving around, telling Brennan what was going on, heard a motor start up. A couple of minutes of a car, questions from Brennan.

Then Nain was back on with me. "What happened,

Molls?"

"Puppets."

"How many?"

"Six."

He cursed. "How did you get away?"

"I fought. I did the mindflayer bit. It was too much."

I waited for the lecture. "Just hold tight. Don't let yourself pass out. I can't feel you if you're unconscious," he said, and I could hear the tension in his voice.

"Okay."

"I'm not too far from where you are."

"Okay."

I kept a look out. The puppet I'd stabbed was still. My eyes started to close.

"I see two cars, blocking the street. Are you near there?" Nain asked.

"Yeah, further down the street," I answered. "I see your headlights, I think. Thanks for coming."

"Anytime."

The truck came to a stop near where the puppets had blocked the street, and Nain and Brennan jumped out and jogged toward me. I stood up, slowly. Nain's eyes were on me the entire time. Brennan looked over the area, alert.

His gaze landed on the puppet on the ground nearby. "He's dead." Approval in his voice.

"Yes. There are three more a few blocks over. We probably need a clean up," I said to Nain. He just nodded, eyes on me, still.

"You did your mindflayer thing on them? Or did your knife get a workout tonight?" Brennan asked.

"Mindflayer. I tapped myself out with them, or I would have done the same with this one. The Puppeteer's strong."

"Why didn't you just set the fuckers on fire, Molly? They shouldn't even have had a shot like this," Brennan said.

Embarrassment flooded me. "I forgot I could do that. I

don't want to use his powers," I said.

They both came over to me. Brennan took my hand and gave it a squeeze. Nain pulled me into his arms, practically crushing me. "If it's you or them, don't ever hold back. Fry the bastards. Do not be ashamed of what you are," he murmured into my hair. I rested my head against his chest, slumped against him. I closed my eyes for a second.

Opened them, and saw the two puppets I'd pepper sprayed coming at us, guns aimed at us.

"Down!" I said, shoving Nain and Brennan down and out of the way, just as the bullets would have struck them. I took three to the stomach instead, molten metal tearing through my body, ripping me to shreds. I bent double, fell, very aware of blood streaming from my body.

I heard Nain's bestial growl, felt fur next to me as Brennan shifted into his preferred form, a huge black cat.

They ran toward the puppets.

I heard one of the puppets scream a little girlie scream, and I would have laughed if I wasn't leaking my guts all over the sidewalk. Growls and shouts pierced the night as I lay there. I could feel my body healing itself, skin slowly, slowly knitting together, shredded organs becoming whole again. It burned like a son of a bitch, and between the burning in my body and the throbbing in my head, I felt like I was being torn apart from the inside out. My eyes closed. I couldn't stay conscious much longer. Blood loss was making me shake. Cold.

Panther Brennan loped back to me. I saw blood glistening on his muzzle, his paws. He looked down at me with blue eyes that were completely Brennan, and shifted back. Nain was on my other side, blood splattering his shirt, his arms. He knelt next to me and started checking my stomach as Brennan stood guard.

Nain pulled at my top to see my stomach, and I tried to push at him, reflexively, remembering the way the puppets had done the same thing. He must have seen something in my eyes. Something murderous thundered in his gaze, and he shook his head. "I'm not going to hurt you, Molls. I just want to see if you're still bleeding."

I still kept my hands on his.

"I promise."

I let go of his hands, and he moved my shirt up, just enough to see the bullet wounds.

"Three times? Holy shit. Anyone else would be a corpse."

"Score one for self-healing."

"You're still hurt."

"Mostly my head now. My body burns when it's healing."

He nodded. "Your skin is on fire. Feels like you have a really high fever."

"I'll cool down when I'm done healing. I'm nearly done bleeding."

He nodded, pulled my shirt back down. "Nice ink," he said, and I was aware he was just trying to keep me conscious.

"Thanks." I blushed. Silly. I hadn't expected anyone, ever, to see the tattoo of Mjolnir I had on my hip.

"Didn't know you were a Thor fan." *Keep talking, Molly. Don't go to sleep.*

I could have cried when I heard his voice in my mind. My powers were not gone. I hadn't burned out completely.

I swallowed, fought back the tears. "I am. But Mjolnir has its own measure of power and symbolism."

"Tell me."

"Protection. Defensive power."

"When did you get it?"

"When I was seventeen."

Nain knew why. He'd seen the whole thing, every part of it, in my mind. He met my eyes, understanding written there. "We need to get you a hammer."

I laughed, and it hurt. I grimaced and stopped. We sat in silence for a few minutes, Brennan still standing guard.

My body started to cool a little. "I think we can go now," I said.

Nain pulled me up, lifted me in his arms. I tried to shove him away, embarrassed that he thought I needed to be carried like a baby.

"Let me take care of you. Just this once," he murmured close to my ear. "You saved us. Let me do this." I stopped shoving. Too tired to really push it, anyway. Nain threw Brennan his keys, and climbed in, settling me on his lap, arms tight around my body.

Brennan drove. I drifted in and out of consciousness.

I wasn't aware of getting to the loft, of being carried into a room, being cleaned up, and tucked in tight.

CHAPTER ELEVEN

I woke up wrapped in Nain's arms, his legs tangled with mine, his chest to my back. The bedroom was just beginning to brighten with pre-dawn sunlight. I faced a wall of windows, grayish-pink sky.

I should get up. Shove him away, I told myself. I have no business here.

No business feeling warm and safe—something I never would have thought I'd feel around Nain, of all people.

I started to sit up and push his arm off of me. He put it around me tighter, pulled me toward him again.

"Stay," he murmured.

"I shouldn't be here. Or you shouldn't be here. One or the other." I started to get up again.

"Just stay," he said again. And I did. Too tired. I closed my eyes and drifted off.

When I woke up again, the sun was shining brightly and I could hear the television on in the living room. Nain and I were still in the same place, same position, but he was awake. I could sense it.

"Can you explain something to me?" I asked quietly, hating to break the relative peace. Who knew when we'd have a moment when we weren't at each other's throats again?

"If I can," he said, and I was reminded again of stone grating against stone.

"My powers were always pretty much the same. Always. And then you came into my life and now nothing is the same. Why?"

He was quiet for a minute. "I think, if we'd met sooner, you would have figured your powers out sooner. You met someone like you, and it woke something inside. You didn't know what you were, or that there were beings like us out there. It wasn't so impossible anymore."

"But it was always there?"

"Yeah. Like when you first manifested your ability to control with your mind. That power was always there. Under stress and crazy ass situations, we discover how far we can really be pushed. And a demon meeting another demon for a first time…that's always crazy, because we instinctively see each other as a threat."

"Well, meeting you was definitely stressful," I said. We were quiet for a while.

"Do you think I'm done discovering crazy shit about myself?"

He laughed then. "I have the feeling that if you haven't manifested a power by now, you probably don't have it."

"Good."

We stayed like that a while, and I became very, very aware of his strong chest pressing against my back, his body and mine touching at every possible point. I patted his arm. "Time to get up. We really shouldn't be here."

He held for a second, and then let go.

I was surprised to feel disappointment. From him, and, even weirder, from myself.

He stayed where he was. I sat on the edge of the bed. I was fully healed. No aches. Even my head had stopped pounding. My power coursed through my body, and I felt so powerful I probably could have taken flight if I wanted to. Alive. Fully alive. Full.

Then it dawned on me, and I turned to glare at Nain. "You sneaky son of a bitch."

"You were starving. One night with me, and you're fully fed. I'll take that as a compliment, Molls," he said, laying back and folding his hands behind his head. I hated myself for blushing.

"I didn't want to feed from you...is that what this was?" I asked, gesturing at the bed.

"You needed to be fed. I needed to sleep. Lucky for you, I'm even pissed off when I'm sleeping."

"It required you to be wrapped around me like that?" I asked, getting out of bed.

"No."

"No?"

"That was for me. You got something, I got something."

"What did you get?" I asked, folding my arms across my chest.

"I got to sleep pressed up against your pert little ass all night."

I shook my head. "You are something else."

"Would have been a lot more fun if we were awake. Maybe next time," he said, getting out of bed and heading into the bathroom.

This all felt WAY too intimate all of a sudden. Waking up together, hearing him brushing his teeth and moving around in the bathroom. He came out and I stalked to the bathroom, slammed the door behind me. I heard him opening and closing drawers, grumbling to himself in the bedroom.

"There's a t-shirt in there if you want it," he shouted to me through the bathroom door.

I cleaned myself up again, swished some of Nain's mouthwash around my mouth. Ran my fingers through my hair and put it back up again, before shrugging out of the huge t-shirt I barely remembered pulling on the night before and pulling the black t-shirt Nain had left for me over my head. His scent surrounded me immediately; cinnamon, sunshine, something spicy that I couldn't define. My stomach did a funny little twist that I tried to ignore.

The shirt went down to my knees. I felt like a child wearing it. I tucked it into my last spare pair of pants. I'd need to buy more clothes, again.

This shit was getting expensive.

I left the bathroom. Nain was still there, sitting in the bed. We looked at each other.

"I need to get home," I said, looking away from him.

"Or you could stay and play," he said.

"You are in a mood today, aren't you?" I said, biting my thumbnail.

He stood up, walked toward me. There was something in his eyes that made my heart pound, turned my legs to jelly. I backed up, reflexively, and my ass hit the bathroom door behind me. He kept coming toward me, closer, until he was inches from me, towering over me. He put a hand on either side of my shoulders, looked at me with such intensity it made my breath catch in my throat.

"Yeah. I am definitely in a mood. You were nearly taken last night. Because you went out, alone and unprepared, and made a bunch of fucking rookie mistakes that could have gotten you killed, or worse. Maybe you'd be better off warming my bed than trying to play the superhero."

I glared up at him, shoved him back. "I….you……" I couldn't even form a sentence.

"What the hell have we spent all this time on? What about control? What about thinking before you just throw your power around? Brennan was right: you should have fried the fuckers before they even got close to you."

"I was focused on getting away from the six — SIX assholes chasing me. Fighting wasn't my first thought," I shouted. My power filled me, and when I shoved him this time, he went flying across the room. It was the first time

I'd been able to do that in months.

He pulled himself away from the cracked plaster wall and stalked toward me. "No? They would have done worse than kill you, Molly," he shouted, and his eyes burned fiery red, and the building shook under the intensity of his power. Mine rose in response to the threat, and the pressure built so high it burned. "You want to be a puppet? You want to be some fucking madman's plaything?"

"Isn't that what I already am?" I shouted.

Nain punched the wall next to me, and chunks of plaster and brick went flying. "You think so?" he asked, and his voice went low. Never a good sign. He closed in on me. "You think I'm the dangerous one?"

I glared up at him, determined not to show him the effect he was having on me.

We stood there, staring each other down. His eyes burned, and he lowered his face to mine, claimed my mouth with a ferocity that should have terrified me.

Something in me, my demon, whatever it was, exalted in the crush of his lips to mine. Something told me to respond, to give in, to let myself enjoy what a large part of me very much wanted.

I have this tendency to be on the stubborn side. And, you know, to not react well to insults and threats.

I tried to shove him, and he didn't move.

I bit his lip. Hard. He jumped back and wiped a hand across his mouth, smearing the blood I'd drawn. His eyes still glowed, and, whether he was stuck wearing a mortal skin or not, he was all demon at that moment, as his power and rage coursed over me.

"Are you afraid, little girl?" he asked, licking the blood away.

I glared at him.

"Your fear is so good. You don't scare often, but when you do, it's addictive." I tried to control myself, tamp my fear down. He responded in kind, the light in his eyes lessening, until he looked more like a man, and less like a demon.

Still felt all demon to me, though.

"Play time is over," I said.

"So soon?" He took a few steps away, visibly making an effort to calm himself. He took a deep breath. I felt his anger draw back a little more. "I'm sorry." Another deep breath, another step back. "You need to be better. Stronger. Smarter. The enemy is not fucking around anymore. He made that clear with last night's attempt."

"You know a lot more about all of this than you've been letting on," I said. "What haven't you told me?"

I sensed for him, then. The jumble of emotions running through him. Rage, always. More today than usual. Desire. Again, nothing new, but something I didn't want to think about too much. Guilt.

Lots of it.

"What's happening?" I asked.

He sat back down on the bed, and I sat next to him. Back to business. He took another breath and raked his hand through his hair. "You were asking about your powers seeming to appear out of nowhere. Meeting me did that. You can blame me if you want. And it's no coincidence everyone's finding out about you now," he said. "I was following you for a while, trying to gauge what you were, before we met that night. I had to hope that I got to you before someone else did. But I think that maybe me following you, maybe me meeting you…I think it made you more visible to the other side."

"Who?"

"Remember that night with the imps? You wanted to know who they served."

I nodded. "You didn't want to answer me."

"My enemy. Astaroth. His hands are in everything. The Puppeteer found you because he wanted her to."

"He who pulls the Puppeteer's strings," I murmured. "The imps tried to warn me about someone, but they couldn't say much, because of the enchantment on them."

He nodded again. "He's the reason I stayed here. Demons don't tend to stay put for very long. We don't put down roots. But he's decided to stay here for some reason, so here I am. We've been fighting it out for over two hundred years. He comes here, and he sees a place ripe for his influence. He sows discord, reaps the benefits. And I do what I can to hold it back. He's been quiet for a long time, now all of a sudden, he's making these moves. All this weird shit happening lately? The Puppeteer, the pyro you took out, these fucking werewolves running rampant on the East side? It's all him."

"How? He's just another demon, right? And I'm stronger than him, or the imps wouldn't have come to me. Let's take him out."

He shook his head. "There you go, again. Thinking like that is going to get you killed. You know nothing about him, and you want to smash your way in and try to take him out?" I bit back a retort, and he continued. "You're stronger than he is. But he has centuries of experience. He has all the big bads out there doing his bidding, somehow. He's been biding his time, or you'd have been destroyed or taken already. "

"So, he's after me now," I said.

"The Puppeteer was his first attempt. And you thwarted her, twice. He won't like that. He's going to come after you harder. I've seen him when he wants something. People die. Usually lots of them."

"What does he want with me?" I asked.

He shrugged. "Think about it, Molls. First, you're stronger than him. That's like waving a red flag in front of a bull. Most demons are not as evolved as I am." I snorted, and he smiled, just a little. Ended all too quickly. "He sees a threat. Unless he can control you. If he controls you, then he has a weapon. Imagine the strife he could cause with someone like you out there doing his bidding."

"I'm not anyone's weapon," I said, remembering what

the imp had said. "I'm not his weapon, and I'm not your weapon."

Nain's eyes met mine again. "No, you're not. You've proven to be less-than-obedient. Not a very good weapon."

"Well, at least you're not denying it," I said.

"You know better. You know what I am. I had no problem trying to use you for my own purposes. I'm on the good guys' side. Doesn't mean I'm not a bastard."

"Well, you're a demon. Demons are major assholes."

"Pot, kettle," he muttered. "He'll still want to use you. And he won't even try to reason with you. He'll use every tool at his disposal, witches, spells, torture, whatever, to *make* you do his bidding. You won't have a choice."

I felt a chill go up my spine, tried to ignore it.

"You know we've been fighting a lot. He's upping his game, throwing more at us. He knows we're with you. This is how he works. Create chaos, and when everyone's distracted, he'll make another move against you."

We were quiet for a minute. "I left you alone for as long as I could. I knew you needed to do things your way. I know you like doing things alone. But when I see you the way I saw you last night...tapped out, starving....he was *this* close to having you, and he never should have gotten that close to begin with." Frustration and guilt rolled off of him.

"If you'd maybe told me some of this before...." I said.

He got up and stalked to the windows again. "I thought we had more time," he said. I felt regret coming from him. It hit me like a punch to the gut.

"Meaning?"

He looked at me. "You need to be strong. You need to train. You need to be fully fed, always. You need to learn to control your powers. I've been going easy on you. Not anymore."

"You have?"

"I'm not kidding, Molly. You think you hate me now.

You'll really hate me by the time this is all over."

"I don't hate you," I said.

"You should. Work on that." We were quiet a minute. "We need to train more. I can't stop you from doing what you do. It would be pointless to try. But you need to start being smarter. Stop rampaging into situations, because it's not just going to be street thugs waiting for you anymore."

The next week was brutal. The demon didn't lie.

I went to work, and I went to the loft, and then I went home (sometimes) and crashed. It was like boot camp for monsters, with an extra dash of "I am a complete freaking mess" added to the mix.

Nain upped my training. He and Brennan focused on teaching me how to get out of situations even if my powers failed. How to break a hold even if your captor is much stronger than you. How to disable a man by pinching the right nerve. How to kill with one punch, if I needed to.

And there was sparring between Nain and I. We both needed it. All of the time we were spending together had us at each others throats. From my end, I knew that part of the problem was that every second we spent together added to that funny twist in my stomach, the feeling that I should run as fast and as far away as I could despite how much I wanted to stay.

Two out of the five days, I woke up with his big body wrapped around mine after I'd crashed at the loft after being up all night fighting big bads or training. I wavered between hating him and needing him, wanting to destroy him and hoping he'd kiss me again. Which he didn't do, and it made me want to scream, because why did I even want him to anyway?

I was a mess.

And when we sparred, it was the only time any of the tension let up, even for a bit. He was still pissed at me for almost being taken (which seemed really unfair, actually), still full of guilt and all kinds of frustration.

We sparred for hours, both of us full of pent-up energy and aggression. He hit me with everything he had, showed me a few tricks I didn't already know, tried repeatedly forcing his way into my mind. My mental shields held. And he quizzed me.

"Best way to kill a werewolf?" Punch.

"The two things that can actually kill a vampire?" Punch slap.

"Name the four most common spells a witch will use on you. Now." Wrestle, pin.

We fought, endlessly. And when we weren't fighting, we were together helping the team contain the chaos erupting in the supernatural community. And we were planning, and he lectured me about control and using my brain instead of letting my fists take charge.

Friday night, we were fighting again. We were both more irritated than usual. It had been a long week, and there was all kinds of weirdness between us. We'd woken up together again that morning. Something I needed to stop making a habit of, but something I kept letting happen anyway. Tension. Need. My own. His. It was seriously messing with my otherwise sunny disposition.

We sparred on the roof, and we were brutal.

"You know, normal people would just have a good screw and get it over with," Stone said at one point when he came up on the roof to watch us. I blushed, ducked away, avoiding another punch.

A spike of desire, frustration from Nain. "Demons aren't normal," he growled.

"Truer words, brother," Stone said, before eventually wandering back inside.

And we fought some more.

Things got testy a few times. At one point, we both did our demon thing and made the building quake. The rest of the team came up to see what was going on, and Brennan got between us.

"The last thing we need is for you two to kill each

other. Knock it off!" he shouted, holding me back and away from Nain.

"Brennan. I want this. Back off," I said, breathless and trying to get back at Nain.

"And what about him? He doesn't have a healing ability, Molly," Brennan said.

I stared at him, laughed. "You're afraid that I'm going to hurt him? Look at him!"

"Brennan," Nain said. "Molly needs this. I need this. You wouldn't understand."

"Fucking crazy demons," Brennan muttered, stalking back into the loft. The rest of the team followed. We went back to fighting.

Despite what I'd said to Brennan, I was actually being careful. I knew when I was hurting him. There was a threshold I wouldn't cross, no matter how much I wanted to. And even though he couldn't sense emotions like I could, I knew he was doing it, too. I was learning control, from the master. And it was necessary. It wouldn't be easy for one of us to seriously hurt the other, but it was a possibility, and more possible the longer we fought.

The fact of the matter was, we made each other stronger. He fed off of the pain he caused me, and I fed off of both the pain I caused him and his ever-present anger. What looked like the two of us killing each other felt like a driveway game of hoops to us.

If you ignored the blood and bruises.

He finally called it quits, and we sat, side by side, exhausted and sweaty, on the old-fashioned glider on the shady side of the roof. He was so tense. So frustrated. Just being near him set my teeth on edge.

"Would you put a lid on it?" I said after gulping some water. "I can't believe you're still this tense after all that."

He didn't answer. If anything, he felt more frustrated.

"What is it? You're even angrier today than usual," I said, tugging at the side of his shirt to get him to look at me. And when he did, the intensity in his eyes floored me.

"Everything. We're running out of time."

"I know Astaroth seems to be throwing more at us, but…"

"He is. I've seen this with him before. He's trying to find our weak points, figure out how we work."

"It's not just Astaroth, though," I said quietly.

He just looked at me. "You know what it is," he finally answered.

"We're spending too much time together."

"Yeah." We were both quiet for a minute. "So why is it that I can't make myself stay away from you?" he asked.

I didn't answer. It was something I'd asked myself about a thousand times over the past week. No matter how much shit he dealt, no matter how surly he was, no matter how much he pissed me off, the one place I wanted to be was near him.

One more thing I didn't want to think about too closely.

We were silent, rocking back and forth on the glider, letting the cool early evening breeze dry our sweat and cool our bodies.

"You need to know more about Astaroth," he said.

"Tell me." I was grateful for the change of subject.

And he did. About witch covens throughout the city, about werewolf packs, forsaken shapeshifters (those who turned their backs on the nobility of their race for their own gains). About lone vampires throughout the city, the Puppeteer and her people. How he thought they might fit into Astaroth's organization. How hard it was to pinpoint anything, because Astaroth was very good at keeping a lid on things. How frustrating it was, because the best he and Ada had were guesses about who was really important in the organization, and who wasn't. How irritating it was that it all lead back to Astaroth, and they had yet to hear even a whisper about where he was.

By the time he stopped talking, my head was spinning.

"So much more out there than I realized," I said. He

nodded.

"Do you see now, why I'm telling you that you have to be smarter? They're working together. One person, even if she's you, can't beat that."

"Oh, ye of little faith," I muttered.

"It has nothing to do with faith. If I didn't believe in you, you wouldn't be here. No one, no matter how well trained they were, could stand against them alone. It's just too much. And you don't have to do it alone. You have me."

The words made my stomach twist.

You have me.

We sat in silence for a while. His thigh was pressed against mine, and I could feel each muscle flex against my skin as he rocked the glider back and forth. His arm laid across the back of the seat, behind me. He twisted a lock of my hair around his finger, something he did almost out of habit. The tension we'd managed to break by fighting was only building again the longer we sat together.

My mind was going to places it shouldn't go.

I moved over a little. "I'm full," I murmured.

"All work and no play, Molls," he said, voice low. How was it possible for someone to set your body on fire with nothing more than a few words?

I blushed. "Stop."

He was quiet for a second. Frustration spiked. "Tell me you don't feel it, too. Tell me you're not almost out of your mind lately. Tell me you're not the least bit curious to find out how damn good it could be between us."

"It would not be a good idea," I said automatically. "If nothing else, it will end badly."

"Probably. We're demons. All I know is I can't stop thinking about you. I try, but it's pointless. You're addictive."

I felt my face flush hotter. "My demon. Not me. Remember?"

"Bullshit."

"Your words," I reminded him.

"I lied."

"We're getting off the subject. We need to focus," I said.

"You're just using me for my rage," he said, meeting my eyes. Humor there. Holy shit the effect just his eyes had on me.

Down, girl.

I tried to shake it off, cool him down. "And as my own personal punching bag."

"Yeah, but that only turns me on more. You're hot when you're in a demonic rage."

My stomach somersaulted. I shook my head. "You're in a mood again. Rein it in, devil boy."

He smiled. Then he tangled his fingers into my hair and pulled me toward him. And when his lips met mine, when he pressed my body to his, when he set me on his lap, kissed me senseless and marked my throat with his teeth over and over again, I did the same to him. And finally, I held nothing back.

A couple of hours later, long after the sun had set, I disentangled myself from Nain and headed down to my car. I wasn't ready for what was obviously on his mind. On my mind. Not just yet.

The demon could *kiss*.

Good Hades.

I had that feeling again that I could fly if I only set my mind to it. I was full of power, I was strong, I was giddy. Everything in the part of my brain that was still sane was screaming at me that this was stupid, that it would only end badly, because, duh, demons, and I wouldn't come back from it unbroken.

I ignored that part of my brain, for once in my life.

So I was grinning when I stepped out of Nain's

building and into the parking lot. Stone and Brennan had brought my car over from my house earlier in the week, so I'd have it if I needed it. Veronica had forgiven me, grudgingly, for ducking out on her. When I got to my car, Brennan was standing there, arms crossed, leaning against the driver's side door.

"Brennan," I said, cocking my head to the side. "Something you need?"

"How did training go?" he asked, and the venom in his voice surprised me.

"You saw," I said.

He just looked at me. Angry, disappointed. Jealous?

"Bren…" I began.

"Just don't," he said. "I don't even know what I'm doing here."

"We're friends, Brennan. There was never even the possibility for more," I said, as gently as I could.

"You could have told me that before," he said.

"I didn't realize it was necessary. I didn't know—"

"You can read emotions and you didn't know? You're pretty shitty at it, then."

"I read it as flirting. I knew you were attracted to me. I didn't expect this."

"So, what? That's it?"

I just stared at him. "How did I miss this?" I asked, myself more than him.

He just glared at me. I could feel it, then. I'd hurt him, more than I ever would have guessed.

"Brennan, it's always been Nain," I said, blushing, knowing the words were true as they left my lips. "Always. As much as I hate him sometimes, as much of a bastard as he is…it's him."

"Because of the demon thing?"

"That, and everything. Whatever he is, it's part of me and I'm part of him. I didn't realize it fully until I said it just now, but, yeah. He belongs to me."

"How nice for you," he muttered.

"Don't do this," I begged. "You're a good, powerful, gorgeous man. You have women throwing themselves at you just walking down the street. I'm the last thing you need."

"Just forget it," he said, turning and walking back into the building.

I was watching him storm into the building, when the imp leader popped out of the Barracuda.

"Hey," I said to him.

"Mistress. Lost girl. East Side imp brigade reports intel that she's in a house in Indian Village."

"Normals, or something else?"

"Vampire."

"Just one?"

He nodded. "Still might want to call demon skin," he said, ears twitching. "Vampires nasty."

I glanced at the building. "I can handle one vampire," I said.

The imp's disbelief was evident on his face. "As Mistress says," was all he said. We got into the car and headed toward Indian Village.

I circled the neighborhood, driving past the house twice. This was a ritzy neighborhood. The homes were large, well-tended. Expensive cars sat in the driveways, and the word "manicured" aptly described everything from the lawns to the people. I'd noticed a private security car driving around. I'd have to avoid that. The last thing I needed was to have to answer questions about what I was doing sneaking around in this neighborhood, wearing all black.

A house like this was trickier than the dumps I usually had to make my way into. One like this could have alarms. Hell, that was probably a given. Especially if the person living there had something to hide. Like a girl.

I parked the car a couple of blocks away, in the parking lot of a little neighborhood coffee shop. I got out and disappeared into the night, jumping fences and making sure I avoided the security squad, making my way back to the brick Tudor where, right this very moment, someone might be living or dying solely on the whim of a sicko creature of the night.

Times like this, when I was getting ready to run into the unknown, I felt more alive than at almost any other time, especially until I'd met Nain. Rage filled me, adrenaline pumped through my veins, and I could feel my power singing within me. My body felt loose. It was the only time I felt normal.

Man, I was one screwed up chick.

I got into the back yard and crept around the house, listening. I could hear a television on somewhere on the first floor. Probably the family room. Or, what did rich people call them…dens? Maybe in the den.

I went around the back. A window was open, letting in the cool night breeze. I listened outside, heard nothing. Cutting the screen and climbing in was simple. This was ridiculously easy.

I was in a bedroom. Dark and empty. I stood and listened, let my eyes adjust to the darkness. The den was across the hall.

"I hear you in there. You might as well come in here talk to me, Angel," a male voice said. And now I knew what a vampire felt like; an energy signature so smooth, so powerful, that it was easy to see how the Normals succumbed to their charms so readily.

I held my knife and walked out of the room and into the den. The imps were still following me. "Sure about this, Mistress?" leader imp asked in a raspy whisper.

I nodded. "Too late now to turn back."

We walked into the den. The vampire was sitting on a dark red wingback chair. He was not a bad looking fella, for an undead parasite. Rather handsome, actually, with wavy brown hair and dark eyes. Pale skin. Fangs.

"Your little network works quickly, doesn't it?" he asked, folding his hands in his lap.

"Yeah, well. We try."

"It's an imperfect system, it would seem. There are no girls here. Well, there weren't until you arrived," he said, smiling.

Oh, shit. I exchanged glances with leader imp. "We been set up, Mistress," he said, shame flooding through him.

"It was easy. Start a rumor or two, get the right people talking. I knew I could count on your imp army to carry word to you." He was still smiling. I surveyed my surroundings, planning, always planning. "Are you afraid? You are." He smiled again as if we were discussing the weather.

"Nah. I'm just disgusted by your decorating choices. Very old lady," I said, still looking around.

He laughed, though I felt irritation coming from him. He wanted me afraid, trembling. Good luck with that, buddy. I'd be afraid later.

"So, now what? Shouldn't there be organ music or something playing, Dracula?"

"Watch it, Angel." Irritation. This one was vain. I could use that. Hopefully.

"So, how are we going to do this? Are you just going to be a nice vamp and admit you made a mistake luring me here? Or am I going to have to hurt you?"

He smiled at me again. His fangs grew. "Oh, I think we should play a while. I can't keep you, unfortunately. Reward to collect and all, but I bet your blood would be spectacular," he said. "I'm sure Astaroth won't begrudge me a little taste." And he got up and charged at me, faster than I would have thought possible.

I grabbed a heavy marble ugly candlestick thing off of a nearby table and swung it at him, Detroit Tigers style, just as he reached me. I made contact, and my arms jerked with the impact. He fell down, but was right back up again. His head was bleeding, but he shook it off and sprung at me again. I kicked out, catching him in the gut. Note to self:

have Brennan teach me more martial arts when he's done being pissed at me. Those kicks came in damn handy, I thought as I watched the vampire fly back against the expensive mahogany bookcases.

I advanced on him, swung the candlestick at him again while he was down, and he caught my wrist in mid-swing. I kicked him between the legs, and he let go of my arm. While he was bent double, I brought the candlestick down on the back of his head, twice. The second time dropped him.

I didn't waste any time in binding his wrists behind him and his ankles together with the zip ties. I had no illusions that they would hold him forever. Vampires were strong, and I'd gotten lucky. I needed to remember to start carrying silver or garlic or something with me.

Vampires. Holy shit.

I added an additional zip tie to both his wrists and ankles. Then I glanced at him one more time and crept through the house. I'd make sure he didn't have any snacks stashed anywhere before I left. The first floor yielded nothing, as did the second floor.

I peeked in at him, noted that he was still out, then headed down to the basement.

Nothing. Well, that much was a relief.

"Gotta go, Mistress," the leader imp said, pulling on my pant leg. "Should have left already."

"I know. I had to be sure. We're going."

Then, of course, I heard footsteps on the basement stairs. I cursed myself for not moving faster. My life was like one of those horror movies where you're yelling at the girl "no, no, don't go in the basement" and she does it anyway. Dumb, dumb, dumb. The imps shrunk back, giving me a fearful glance.

I grabbed the candlestick again. It had worked wonders so far.

CHAPTER TWELVE

The vampire was now visible on the stairway. And the further down he came, the better I was able to see him.

And he carried a sword.

Candlestick-wielding mindflayer versus sword-wielding vampire. Great.

I tried using my mental power, even though, from what little I knew, I didn't think they'd work on vamps. "You want to drop the sword now," I said, filling my voice. He simply laughed and shook his head.

"Mortal mind powers have no effect on the undead, bitch," he said, coming slowly toward me. "It's convenient that you made your way down here. Blood is so hard to get out of the upholstery."

Keep him talking. "It's ugly furniture anyway. The blood would be an improvement." He kept coming at me. "That's quite a bump there, Fangy. Poor baby," I mocked.

"I can see why you have so many enemies," he growled. "It will be a pleasure to have you unconscious for a while."

"Well, I'll just stand here, trembling in fear. Oh, wait. No. No, I won't."

"What are you going to do, mortal?"

"I am going to kick your pale ass so hard you won't know which hole to piss out of." Then I thought a second. "Wait. Do vampires even have to piss?"

"We do not."

"Oh, well. You get the point." And I lunged at him, surprising him, and he met my candlestick arm with his sword, sweeping the candlestick easily aside.

After a few more hits, it became clear that getting into a fight with a vampire was among the dumbest ideas I'd ever had.

He kept sweeping the sword at me, and the best I could do was try to time it to knock the sword away. I earned a series of cuts along my arms, shoulders, and sides, and I could feel my blood soaking through my clothing. I was weakening. I was strong, when I was fully focused. But a lot of my power was going toward closing and healing the wounds I was getting. And I was accumulating wounds faster than I could heal them.

He was pushing me back, toward the wall, trying to corner me. His fangs were fully extended now, and he had a crazed, hungry look in his eyes. All the blood.

He struck at me, hard, with the sword, and I backed up, trying to miss the blade that was aimed for my neck. I ended up overbalancing, and tripped over a crate on the floor behind me, fell back, hard, onto the concrete floor.

He laughed, gleefully, like a madman, and tossed the sword aside, leaping on top of me. I struggled, but vampires are freakishly strong, and I was weak from healing. I needed more energy. I cursed my stupidity.

Fire. Fire and vampires didn't mix. I tried to call my fire as the vampire lowered his face to my throat.

Nothing. Too weak.

Stupid. So freaking stupid, I cursed myself.

I felt his fangs pierce the side of my neck, in slow, agonizing detail. I could feel the instant fang punctured skin. I could feel my blood start to trickle, felt each pull as he began to drink from me. My neck and shoulder were on fire.

I started to panic. Tried to call my fire again. Nothing.

Irony. My healing ability may have just helped seal my doom.

Thinking became harder.

I could feel my heart start to slow.

Thump.

I remembered Nain's teeth on my neck, my collarbone, just hours ago. Ecstasy.

Thump.

Please, fire?

Thump.

Please.

Thump...

Please, fire? I begged as the vampire kept drinking.

I thought of all the things I still needed to do: destroy Astaroth. Make things right with Brennan. Learn who my parents were. Feed my dogs. Let Ada teach me about defensive gems.

Many things involving Nain.

Thump.

Please.

Just a spark?

Thump.

And then I felt it. Even as my heart slowed more, a flicker. Just a little.

Please.

I opened my hand. Willed the fire forth.

A tiny, perfect ball of fire appeared in my hand, and I smashed it into the vampire's back. Flames crept along the back of his shirt.

He ripped his fangs out of my neck, and I nearly passed out from the pain of it. He screeched, flinging himself away and trying to put the fire out. He rolled, and, eventually the flames died out.

His back was burnt, blackened, and terror, anger, flooded from him. Panic. The basement smelled like cooked flesh. I stood up said a silent thank you to whichever gods had helped me remember my fire.

I still hated using it. Stolen treasure. It still felt dirty flowing through my body. But it had saved my life this time. And I wasn't done yet.

I called forth another ball of fire. I was dizzy, determined not to let him see how weak I still was. My body had resumed healing itself, slowly. The gaping wound in my neck, where he'd been biting me, was the worst of it. The burning as I healed was almost too much.

No way I'd let this parasite see that.

"I believe you said you wanted to play," I said.

He snarled at me, but cowered into a corner.

"Where is Astaroth?"

He hissed at me, and I bobbled the fire in my hands.

"You know where he is. You were going to bring me to him. So where is he?"

"You're going to kill me anyway," he said. "I'm not telling you a thing, demon bitch."

I felt the leader imp standing next to me. "Get Nain, please," I said softly.

"Wifey already gone to get demon skin," he said. "Heard you say his name."

"Excellent." Then I glanced at him. "I didn't know you two were married. How nice."

He shrugged. "Five hundred and twenty seven years."

"Wow."

"Yes."

We stood that way a long time, me holding fire in my palm, the vampire cowering and glaring at me from the corner, and leader imp watching my back.

"You have a name?" I finally asked the imp.

"Bashiok. Wifey is Dahael."

"Sorry I didn't ask before," I said, still watching the vampire.

"Mistress is the first to bother asking."

"Demons are jerkfaces," I said.

The imp stayed silent, but I sensed humor.

It wasn't long before I heard heavy footsteps up above, felt Nain's presence. Dahael came scampering down the stairs first, followed by Nain. I felt my power growing, fed just by being in his presence. I devoured him with my eyes. I watched him as he took in the sight of me and my shredded, bloody clothes, surveyed the basement floor covered in drying, sticky blood. Rage flooded through him, and when his gaze finally landed on the vampire now pitifully cowering in the corner, I could feel how much he wanted to destroy the creature.

"Molls," he said, cool and calm on the outside. Only the muscle tic in his clenched jaw gave him away. And I only recognized it because I'd seen him pissed off so often.

Usually, at me.

"Hey." I nodded toward the vampire. "Vlad here knows where Astaroth is. He was going to turn me over to him. He won't tell me, but then it occurred to me that it might be better if you ask him." *I tried getting into his head. I'm still nearly tapped out. The fire and healing are all I can manage.*

Nain looked at me, raised his eyebrow. *It makes me hot when you get all tactical like this.*

I bit back a grin.

He hurt you.

Yeah. It was gross.

I'm going to enjoy hurting him. I am the only one who gets to bite you.

I blushed, felt my body responding to him, to the desire, rage, and adrenaline running through him.

I looked at Nain again, met his eyes. I nodded toward the vampire, and Nain gave me a nod in return.

"Okay, bloodsucker. Here's the deal." He spotted the sword the vampire had tossed aside, went over and picked it up, weighed it in his hand. My blood still stained the blade. "You know things. You'll tell us. My blade can end it quickly if you behave yourself. But the demoness there? You've really pissed her off. And she's not someone you want to piss off. Looks like you got a little taste of her wrath already. She can fuck you up real bad. And she can do it over and over again, for as long as it takes for us to learn what we want. And you know what I am. I'll know if you try to lie to me."

The vampire snarled. "Screw you. She's dead, just as much as I am."

I took a breath, swallowed against the sick feeling in my stomach. Now that he was here, and it was clear what would happen to the vampire, I almost felt bad for the bloodsucker.

Molly. He was dead anyway. Don't.

This is wrong. Just kill him. I shouldn't have called you.

He knows things. Do you want to be surprised like this again?

I didn't answer.

"He knows where to find her, demon. He will take her, or one of us will make a gift of her, but either way her time is up."

That is not acceptable. Hate me later, but this fucker is telling us what he knows.

"So where is he?" Nain asked the vampire, glancing at me.

"She was delectable, by the way. Intoxicating."

I felt rage course through Nain.

"Can't say I was as impressed with you," I muttered.

"Astaroth is really going to have fun with you, mindflayer."

I walked over to where he was huddled, in pain. "Tell us what you know," I said softly. "He'll end it quickly."

He just glared at me. Then he laughed. "She doesn't have the stomach for it. You chose a weak weapon, Nain Rouge."

Then Nain met my eyes. "Go upstairs, Molly."

I nodded, climbed the stairs. My imps trailed me, and I could feel Nain's eyes on me as I went.

I waited in the living room with the imps. I paced, listened to the grunts and screams coming from the basement. A few shouts. Nain's rage permeated the very air around me. He was frustrated. I felt victory a few times from him. I guessed he was learning something. I tried not to think about what he was doing.

It went on for hours. Eventually, I lost all sense of the vampire, and I heard Nain climbing the stairs. I glanced at the imps. "You should go outside." Bashiok and Dahael nodded, scurried out the front door.

Nain walked into the living room. He was covered in pale blood. Not his. He met my eyes, and I saw him glance at my neck. It had not finished healing yet, but at least it wasn't bleeding as much.

"He told me what I wanted to know. He didn't know where Astaroth is, only how to reach him. Who's in his inner circle. It's a start," he said.

I nodded. Felt sick.

"It was necessary. He signed his death warrant the moment he lured you here."

"I know," I said softly. "You liked hurting him."

"Yeah, I did. Just like you like how it feels when you put the hurt on someone." Then he walked up to me, stood in front of me. "But I enjoyed this even more than usual. He made the mistake of trying to take something of mine."

"I'm not yours," I said, glaring up at him. "Not your anything. Not your weapon—"

"Are we still on this?" he asked, exasperated. "You're not my weapon. I shouldn't have asked you to do that. But you are mine, whether you'll admit it or not."

He closed in on me, and I backed up into the side of the vampire's grand piano. Nain put a hand on each side of my body, caging me in. "You're disgusted by what I did. I get that. I've done worse. And I'll guarantee you that I'll do worse than that before this is all over. I will do what it takes to keep those I care about safe. Anyone messes with Ada, Stone, Brennan, Veronica, they're asking for the pain. And anyone who fucks with you is asking for it, double."

The possessiveness, the anger, the violence he'd just demonstrated…it should have completely disgusted and terrified me. On one level, it did. But the more twisted part of me, the part that liked pain and craved fear, the part of me that was all demon — that part liked it. A lot.

He closed in on me, gently kissed my neck where the vampire had injured me. His lips moved over it softly, his tongue lapping at the fresh skin there, and I felt heat pool low in my body, molten need that was just as aroused by what he'd done for me as what he was currently doing to me.

Then, his mouth claimed mine, and I whimpered when he lifted me up onto the piano and pressed his body close to mine. His arms were around me, holding me close to him. Need coursed through him. He nuzzled my neck, sucked at my earlobe.

He nearly took you from me, he thought at me, and I felt something I'd never felt from him: fear. All the crazy shit he'd seen, all the battles we'd fought, and I'd never once felt fear from him.

His fingers dug into my hips, and he kissed me again, hard, rough, full of need and frustration and desperation.

Nain. I could barely breathe, drowning under the sensation of the emotions going through us.

Molly.

I need you. Now.

Surprise ran through him, victory, and before I could even think, he lifted me up and pushed my jeans down my thighs. I kicked them off. He palmed my bottom, scraped his teeth along my jawline as I unzipped his jeans.

He claimed me with one long, hard thrust, growling in triumph. A similar wild sound left my throat, and then I was overtaken by the sensations running through my body, of him pounding into me, his hands and lips, teeth everywhere.

There was nothing gentle in this. It was not slow. It was not sweet. We went at it like the demons we were, more animal than anything else. Rational thought left me. I whimpered and moaned as he filled me, dug my fingernails into the hard muscles of his back and shoulders.

I could hear his every thought, feel his every emotion. We were connected in every way. Two bodies chasing pleasure with abandon; minds, souls entwining in a way I'd never imagined possible.

When he was finished, when we were both sated, exhausted, he drove into me, hard, one last time, bit my lower lip, then stepped back. I slid to the floor on legs that barely seemed capable of supporting me. I pulled my ripped, bloody jeans back on. My hands were trembling, my body aching and weak. Nain seemed to sense it. He walked forward, pushed my hands away gently and went to work putting me back together again.

So good. You were so damn good, Molly.

I glanced up at him, felt my face burn. Had I really just done that? With him? I looked away quickly.

He laughed, low and deep, and stepped closer to me. He folded me in his arms, kissed my lips, my neck, my earlobe, gently. "My name is Bael," he whispered, his breath tickling the sensitive skin near my ear. "My real name. You're the only one in this world or the Nether who knows it."

I wrapped my arms around his neck, nuzzled his cheek and felt coarse hair abrade my cheek. "I think I might be in love with you, Bael. You bastard," I murmured.

He laughed against my neck, and I felt a bolt of pure happiness, victory, run through him. "It's about fucking time, woman. I've been in love with you since the moment I laid eyes on you."

We stood there, folded in each other's arms, leaning against each other. Silent.

The moment of peace was broken by Nain's phone ringing. He nuzzled my neck one more time. "That's Ada's ring. She never calls me unless something's up."

I nodded, started to step back. He dug his phone out of

his jeans pocket, put his other arm around me again and pulled me close. He answered the phone, and his fingers softly trailed up and down my spine. I could hear Ada:

"Nain. The Morningside shifters are causing trouble. They attacked a couple of Normals and all hell broke loose. Stone and I are on our way there, and Brennan and Veronica are coming — they were checking out that lone were we've been hearing about. I tried getting a hold of Molly—"

"She's here," Nain said. "We're on our way." He hung up, put the phone away, then drew me close again. "Ready to go kick some shifter ass?"

I smiled up at him. "Always." He grabbed my hand and led me out of the house. As we raced toward the fight with the shifters, I had a feeling, deep in the pit of my stomach, that this was the last time I'd feel this happy again for a long, long time.

Nain and I arrived at the Morningside neighborhood within minutes. Nain parked the truck, and we both jumped out, ran toward the chaos. Normals were screaming, and the snarls and growls of the shifters cut the night.

"This ain't normal. Even these backward shifters don't do things like this," Nain muttered as we ran. "Be careful."

"Yeah. You know me. Careful," I said. I felt humor from him, and we separated, him heading toward where Stone and Ada were fighting one small group, and me heading toward Brennan and Veronica. They were working together, Brennan feinting, herding the shifters close enough to Veronica so she could grab them. Then she'd do her thing, and, before they knew it, with a single touch they had enough toxins in their bodies to put them in comas. They were lucky she had more restraint than I did.

I ran to where they were, went back to back with them.

"She's here," I heard one of the shifters, who had shifted back into his human form, yell to the others. "The mindflayer bitch is here."

"I really am tired of assholes calling me that," I muttered.

Veronica glanced at me and grinned. Then she noticed my torn, bloody clothes.

"Holy crap! Rough night?" she asked, grabbing another shifter that Brennan hurtled toward her.

"Fucking vampire," I said, going into a nearby shifter's mind and making him go to sleep.

"Ew."

"Seriously."

"Did he get a taste?" Veronica asked, laughing and laying out another shifter.

"Yeah," I said, grunting as I focused an energy blast at a shifter who was running toward me. "For the record, I taste good."

We cleared out our group of shifters, and Brennan shifted back. "TMI, Molly," he said, winking at me. I shook my head, but couldn't quite stop myself from grinning. Relief that whatever weirdness was between us earlier seemed to be gone.

The three of us headed to where Nain and Stone were protecting Ada as she worked her shielding spell. Someone had managed to call the police, and I saw two squad cars heading for us.

"Molly," Nain shouted, pointing at them. I nodded, walked toward the cars, hands up so they'd know I meant no harm.

The officers got out of their cars, gathered around me to hear what was going on. It only took seconds to convince them that there was nothing going on, to go back and report that it was a false alarm.

"These aren't the shapeshifters you're looking for," Brennan murmured behind me, and I laughed. "Jedi mind trick. I am so jealous."

I turned and looked at him, and he grinned. Everything seemed to be dying down. I was about to respond with some dorky Star Wars joke, but I glanced over toward

Veronica and saw a shifter lunging at her from behind.

"Veronica!" I shouted, running toward her. Too late. The shifter grabbed her from behind, holding her hands so that she couldn't touch him and defend herself.

"Stop, mindflayer," the shifter holding Veronica said. "Don't move, and if I feel you or the other demon in my head, she's dead."

I stared at him. Thinking. I felt the other shifters gathering around us. Stone was holding George back.

"And we know that fucker can go invisible. You just stay where we can see you," the shifter said to George. Then he looked back at me.

I sized him up. He was about Veronica's height, maybe five ten or so. Strong. Dark hair and a full beard. I stood there, crossed my arms. I could set the bastard on fire. Could be enough to distract him enough to let go of Veronica.

"If you do anything to me, there are three of my friends with guns perched in the area. If I'm in trouble, they'll shoot her brains out. And if not her, then one of you other assholes. She's the only one with a healing power," he finished, nodding toward me.

"You seem to know a lot about us," I said, keeping my voice calm. It wouldn't do to freak any of them out. I didn't doubt that there were guns trained on my friends.

"My boss knows everything about you, Angel."

"Astaroth," I muttered.

"We were almost afraid you wouldn't show. But, I thought…attacking your precious Normals, the Angel would show. And here you are."

"What, do you want a cookie?" I asked, rolling my eyes. I sensed irritation from him. Tension filled the air. His packmates were nervous. Good.

"All you have to do is come with us, quietly. Let us collect our reward, and all of your little friends can go on their way," he said.

"How do I know you won't just have them killed,

either way?"

Molly, no.

Quiet. Wait.

"The only one we're interested in is you."

"What do you get out of this?"

The shifter alpha laughed. "Astaroth will pay very well for you. We'll never have to worry about money again. Have the best of everything. And he's got some powerful allies. This will be the last day we ever have to cower, to hide, in fear of you and that demon asshole coming down on us."

"Maybe if you joined us instead of acting like animals, you wouldn't have to worry about hiding from us," I said.

"Yeah, that was ever a possibility," the shifter alpha said, snorting. "You and him, your little group of vigilantes here. You think you're so much better than the rest of us. I know what you are. I know how demons get strong. You want to believe you're better than us, the fact of the matter is you're the biggest fucking animal here."

I could feel Nain's rage behind me, on my behalf. He really didn't take it well when people insulted me.

"Well, Rover," I said, and felt his irritation spike. "You aren't the only ones who tried to take a crack at me tonight." I held my arms open, showing him the mess my clothes had become. "A vampire over in Indian Village tried it a while ago." I felt fear in his pack mates, had to hold back a smile. "And you see. I'm here. And he's rotting in a basement, minus his head."

No need to tell them who removed his head, I thought at Nain.

You can pay for my silence later, woman, he thought back, humor from him.

More fear. So good. I felt it strengthening me, felt it buzzing through my body. Alive. Fear was a living thing, and it belonged to me.

The beautiful thing about fear, besides the obvious, was that I could feel exactly where it was coming from. I could home in on those feeling it, sense them without having to see them.

There were six of them. The alpha, holding Veronica. The two standing next to him. Three more above: two in the trees behind me, one in a house to my left, on the second floor, peeking out the window.

"So I'm going to give you one more chance, Fido. You and your friends run. Leave my friends alone. And we'll let you live, tonight. If not. I'll send you and your pack to your good buddy Astaroth in a garbage bag." He just stared at me. "Your choice."

He laughed. "What are you gonna do, bitch?" He wasn't going to back down. One on one fighting wouldn't work.

I sent a silent wish that I would not fuck this up.

"This." And I released fire, in five directions, perfect, searingly hot balls of molten death hurtling toward five of our enemies, then I lunged for the alpha, who was still holding Veronica. Screams, terror filled the night as my fire hit its marks. I smiled.

The alpha still held Veronica, tried to run back with her. My friends stood back and watched the shifters burn. My focus was on the alpha.

Molly he's got a– Nain said in my mind. Too late.

The alpha flashed a switchblade, and ran it across Veronica's throat.

It all happened in slow motion.

The surprised look that froze on her face as she was cut open.

The first streams of blood falling onto her pink t-shirt.

Her body going limp.

I snapped out of it and charged at the alpha. When I hit him, Veronica went tumbling from his arms. I used every bit of my strength, bashed his head into the concrete of the street. I went into his mind, made him feel real pain without ever having to lay another hand on him. I tortured him with nothing more than a thought, turned his mind into a prison, his thoughts into weapons. He screamed, a high, terrified scream that cut off when I finally destroyed his mind, tore him apart. Fire ate him from the inside out, and he collapsed into nothing more than smoldering flesh.

When it was done, I turned to where I'd last seen Veronica.

George cradled her limp body in his arms. Her eyes were glassy, empty. Blood still flowed slowly from the wound across her neck, and her legs splayed in a way that made me want to straighten them for her. She'd been such a together, beautiful creature in life. She deserved better than this.

I bit my lip against the rage and loss I was feeling.

My fault. Holy shit she was dead because of me, why the hell did I let this happen?

Nain came up behind me, put his hands on my shoulders. Ada and Stone were hugging each other, crying. Brennan crouched next to George, head bowed.

Don't. This is not your fault, Nain said in my mind.

She's dead because of me. Her blood is on my hands.

Brennan stood up, came to us. He folded me in a huge hug, and when he stepped back, his eyes were red. "Fuckers."

I nodded. Looked at Nain. "You know how to get a message to him, thanks to the vampire, right?"

Nain nodded. I gave him a nod, stalked into one of the now-empty homes, and found a large black garbage bag.

I went around the neighborhood, shoveling the remains of the six shifters into the bag. I ignored my disgust at seeing a stray jawbone here, a hand there. I bagged it all up. It took less than a whole bag. I tied it up, found paper, and jotted a note.

"Molly 7, Astaroth 0. You're next."

I duct taped it to the bag and called Bashiok, Dahael, and six of the other imps, who had gathered as the chaos erupted. "Ask Nain where to deliver this. Leave it there. Be careful." They thumped their fists to their chests, then two of them took the bag and scampered off into the night.

I turned to Nain, met his eyes. "This ends now," I said.

I felt regret, sadness, anger from him. He nodded. "Dead demon."

We all stood, gathered around Veronica's body until Nain's pastor friend, Pastor Balester, came to collect her and prepare her for her burial.

Veronica's burial was not quite what I was expecting. It happened that very night. We all went home, cleaned up, dressed in the customary black. Then we made our way to the large stone church and cemetery that Father Balester served, not too far from my house, actually.

I pulled into the parking lot, which was empty other than Nain's black truck and Stone's Harley. The team was standing around near the wrought iron fence, waiting for me.

I'd seen the team tired. I'd seen them angry, stressed out, frustrated. Seeing them like this, broken and mourning, nearly flattened me. They had lost a sister, a partner. I mourned Veronica's loss. She was the closest thing I'd ever had to a friend. But my pain was nothing compared to theirs. Nain folded me in his arms when I reached him, then I hugged my other team mates. Except for George, who stood apart from everyone else and clearly wanted nothing to do with us.

Within a few moments, Father Balester walked out of the church, dressed in his black vestments. He greeted the team in a subdued, serious manner that immediately made me like the man.

He glanced at me. "Is this your first supernatural funeral?"

I nodded.

He gave a small smile. "They are not much like mortal burials. Seeing my first one when I was young made me believe in what lies beyond. It is the reason I became a priest."

I watched him. Sensed for him. Ah. Power.

"You're something. I don't recognize it, though," I said, still trying to feel for him.

He smiled at me. And then he winked, and where he'd been standing, a majestic oak stood instead. I gaped at it, and watched as the air shimmered and he resumed his human form.

He gave a small laugh. "Earth guardian. We try to clean up the messes the mortals make, try to keep things in balance."

"Must be a hard job," I said, thinking of the steel and concrete that surrounded us.

He nodded. "But a worthwhile one. I've been here since this area was nothing but swampy forests. Things change, but the fight goes on."

"One would think you'd have your hands full enough, without entering the priesthood."

Father Balester smiled. "I serve a very specific community. The Catholic church barely knows I'm here. This church lies on sacred ground, the perfect place to send our brothers and sisters on to what is next."

"And what is next?" I asked, my stomach clenching.

"Judgment. For all of us. The Lord of the Nether judges us all, and decides how we shall spend eternity."

"I thought that was St. Peter," I said. He smiled again. "Each tradition puts its spin on it. It is all the same thing. Only the explanations, the mythology, differ." He paused. "Normals leave this world, and their souls are collected quietly, escorted swiftly to the ever after. But supers...we all have a bit of the Nether in us. You and Nain, being demons, more so than the rest of us, obviously. When supers die, the Guardians come to collect us. The Lord of the Nether decides our eternal fate, and the Furies carry out his judgment. Because we had more power, our judgment in the ever after is much harsher than those who had no power."

"Please don't say 'with great power must come great responsibility.'" I said, smiling.

He laughed. "Spidey's Uncle Ben had it right. Yeah. We've been given gifts, for whatever reason. We are judged swiftly and harshly by the Lord of the Nether. You, a demon, are progeny of the Nether, and will be judged most harshly. When your death comes, you will return to the Nether for eternity. It will not be pleasant."

"Well, this has been a fun talk, Padre," I said.

"Consider it a warning. Use your time here well, Angel."

Father Balester met my eyes one last time, then walked toward the cemetery. Nain took my hand, and we all followed him into the dark cemetery.

It should have been creepy, but it was peaceful. Veronica's body was on the ground, clean and dressed in a simple black gown. Her hands were folded over her stomach. No effort had been made to disguise the wound that killed her. There was no artifice here, no pretense of prettying up the dirty business of death. I respected the Father even more for that.

We sat in silence, and Father Balester began to chant, words I couldn't understand, but could feel down to my soul. A summoning, a request. A hush fell over us.

"I advise you now to say your goodbyes," Father Balester said quietly. "Her soul is about to be freed from its mortal prison. She will be judged by Our Lord of the Nether. May her soul live on in peace."

I looked at Veronica's body. Remembered a sweet woman who'd tried to be my friend. A friend who'd died because of her association with me. I closed my eyes and promised her vengeance, swore it as I felt strange energy begin to surround us, power that washed over me in waves.

I opened my eyes to see the air shimmer near us, and three winged figures flew out of what seemed to be nothingness. These were not angels. There was nothing cherubic about these beings. They were small, maybe four feet tall at the most. Skin, pale white with an otherworldly luster. Compact, powerful bodies. Flowing black hair, eyes that glowed deep red in the night. And wings. Black feathered wings that extended from their backs. Slender arms ended in hands with long, sharp claws. Their faces were so beautiful, I could hardly look away. The three beings landed, soundlessly. I watched them as they surrounded Veronica's body, joined hands, and began chanting, singing words that I couldn't understand but that tugged at my soul just the same. The chanting got louder, more intense. And then I understood:

"We escort thee,
sister, warrior,
to life everafter."

They chanted it over and over again, louder. It was beautiful, and frightening. Awe-inspiring.

I saw the moment Veronica's tether to the mortal world ceased to be. Her body simply winked out of existence, two of the Guardians disappearing with it. The third Guardian paused, then turned to look at me. My heart stilled when her eyes settled on me. She looked me over, then cocked her head to the side. She reminded me of a bird. A deadly, intelligent bird, but a bird nonetheless. She stood like that for several seconds, watching me. Something seemed to satisfy her. She smiled at me, winked, then flapped her wings and took off into the nothingness beyond.

Once she'd left, all was silent and calm. I felt surprise, confusion coming from the beings surrounding me. I looked around to see them all staring at me.

"What?" I asked, crossing my arms.

"She looked at you," Ada said.

"So?"

Father Balester was looking at me intently, as if trying to see whatever the Guardian had seen in me. "They are above those of us on the mortal plane, in every way. I've been doing these ceremonies for almost a thousand years. Never once have I seen a Guardian pay any attention at all to one of us."

I felt cold. "Well, I'm sure that bodes super well for me, then," I said.

We all went our separate ways shortly after. Brennan, Ada, and Stone headed off together in Nain's truck. George raced off in his car, alone. Nain and I drove to my house in my car.

We entered the house wordlessly, headed up to my room. One of the great things about being with someone who can read your mind is that it's very clear to one another what you need. And what we both needed was to be held, to feel safe and not so alone, even if just for a while. I changed into my pajama bottoms and a cami, and he stripped down to his boxers, and we climbed under my bedspread together, locked in each other's arms.

"Why can't I cry? I feel like I should cry over her," I said finally.

Nain's fingers ran up and down my spine. "You have your own way of dealing with things. You're not a crier. Nothing wrong with that." We were quiet again. "You deal with grief by kicking ass."

"I am going to kill Astaroth," I promised.

"Yes. You are. And I'm going to help." I felt that same tension in him whenever we talked about Astaroth. Time to get some answers.

"You know, I get this crazy feeling that there's something you're not telling me," I said.

He was quiet, fingers still trailing up and down my back. I had my face pressed against his chest, feeling his heart beat under my cheek. "There are things I haven't told you," he finally said.

"Tell me."

He was nervous. Regret, anger, sadness coursed through him. Fed me, as always. "Before I changed my ways, I was part of a gang of demons that caused a lot of damage in this area. We killed, destroyed whatever we wanted. We took what we wanted. We vanquished those who stood in our way." He paused, and I felt shame from him.

"I already knew that," I reminded him.

"We were not just an unorganized gang. We had a leader."

"Astaroth," I guessed.

"Yeah. I joined him, because I was attracted to what his demons were doing. They lived a good life. They were strong, feared. I wanted to be one of them. And I was so fucking good at causing terror. He accepted me, gladly. Before long, I was his right hand demon, his second in command. Whatever Astaroth wanted done, I made sure it happened. I had all the power I could have ever wanted."

I tried to imagine him working side by side with the vile creature I'd come to hate, and I couldn't do it. Tried to imagine him planning, plotting with Astaroth.

"But you went a different way, Bael," I whispered, using his real name. He hugged me tightly.

"Yeah. It was a fight to get away from him once I'd decided I was done. Thing was, I was stronger than him, and he knew it. We fought, over and over again once I'd cut my ties with him. You know how demons are. If I wasn't with him, then I needed to be destroyed."

"But he couldn't do it," I said, prodding him on. I felt a strange, primal pride in him. He had been unbeatable. My man.

"He couldn't. And if a demon can't win by strength, he'll try to win by lies. He had a witch cast a spell on me to trap me in a mortal body. He knew it would take most of my power away from me. It was a solid plan on his part."

"Yet, you're still here," I said.

He went silent. "We came to an uneasy agreement after a while. Decided to leave each other alone. He stayed out of my way, and I stayed out of his."

"That doesn't make any sense," I said. "He had what he wanted. You were weak. Everything I know about Astaroth tells me he wouldn't have hesitated to go in for the kill."

He paused, and I felt irritation coming from him. Regret. "I'm sure he had his reasons," he finally said.

"What the hell does that mean?" I asked, exasperated.

"It means, that's all I can tell you about it," he said. "Let's talk about something else."

I sighed. Damn stubborn demon. "What?"

"Us." Nervous.

"What about us?"

"I love you."

"Yeah. I know. I love you, too. Even if you're a stubborn ass," I said.

I felt him shake a little as he laughed. "And you're a real sweetheart yourself, baby." He was quiet a minute. "I love you," he repeated. "You're the only one for me, ever."

I held my breath. He wasn't going to...?

"Demons don't really get married. Not like Normals do, anyway. When we decide to give our bodies and souls to another, we exchange blood, a way of tying us to one another."

I looked up at him. "What does it do?"

"You know how you can sense emotions?" I nodded. "Once we exchange blood, we'll always know how the other is feeling. If one of us should happen to die, the other would know it. If you were in pain, I'd feel it, too."

"Bael," I whispered, staring at him.

"So it's not without its risks. If we do this, and we lose each other for some reason, the one who's left behind is going to do more than mourn. They're going to feel like part of their soul has been torn away. Because it has." Guilt from him.

"What the hell was that?"

"What?"

"You felt guilty about something."

"Damn it, woman."

"Explain."

"I feel guilty about asking you to do something we shouldn't do. We are both on the fast track to the everafter, the way we keep going after the bad guys. Doing this sentences whoever is left to a lifetime of pain. I feel like an asshole for even asking, but I want to feel this connection with you, for however long I can. I'm a selfish bastard."

I reached up and stroked his cheek, felt rough stubble against my palm. "I'd feel a lifetime of pain if I ever lost you, either way. How do we do this?"

He met my eyes, sat up. He sat in the middle of my bed, and sat me on his lap, facing him. He reached down, into the pocket of his pants next to the bed, and pulled a strip of black cloth and a small box out, placed it on the bed next to us.

"Where's your knife?" he asked.

"Nightstand drawer," I said. He reached over and grabbed the pearl-handled switchblade out of the drawer.

He sliced his wrist, and I sliced mine. We pressed our bleeding wrists together, then worked together to bind our wounds, our wrists, together with the strip of black cloth. Then we sat, bound together. My eyes never left his.

I felt the moment his blood entered my body.

"Whoa," I breathed. He let out a contented, satisfied sigh. Peace came to me through our connection, happiness. I could feel his blood, alive and flowing through my veins, pumping through my heart. It was like having him with me, intimately and completely.

"Oh my god," I murmured. He let out a small groan as he felt my blood start to course through his body. His breathing escalated, and I could feel his pulse start racing. Mine did the same. "You're so beautiful, Molly," he said. Then he kissed me, softly, tenderly.

When we finally parted, he unwrapped our wrists. Both

cuts had healed. His blood was sealed inside my body; mine in his. Then he smiled at me and opened the box. He slid a simple hematite band onto my ring finger, then I did the same to him. Our concession to the traditions of the Normal world. A visible sign of our devotion to one another.

"Now, you're officially mine," he said, closing in for another kiss.

"Already was," I whispered just before his mouth met mine. *Always*, I thought at him. And it was the last rational thought I had as we began to comfort each other as only we could.

CHAPTER THIRTEEN

I dropped Nain off at the loft the next morning, and went off on my own despite his irritation and worry over it. I'd taken a few vacation days from my "real" job, and now wondered if I would go back at all. I had a decent amount of money saved up. If things got rough, I could sell the Barracuda. Between my own work finding lost girls and the increased amount of work I was doing with the team due to Astaroth, I could barely face heading into the office any more.

Astaroth. I parked the car near an abandoned church not too far from downtown, got out, and leaned against the driver's side door. I summoned Bashiok and Dahael. I'd realized over the past several weeks that all I really had to do when I wanted them was think their names, and they'd show up pretty quickly. I kept meaning to ask them how they got places as fast as they did, but there never seemed to be any time.

Later.

A few minutes passed, then I saw their squat figures coming toward me. They both bowed when they reached me.

"How did the delivery go last night?"

"Delivered the package to address demon skin gave us.

Left it on the doorstep as Mistress said. We stayed, watched."

"And?"

"Demons took it inside. Later, big boom from inside building," Bashiok said.

Dahael giggled. "Bad demon not happy," she said.

"Good. So does it seem like that is his base?"

Bashiok shook his head. "Meeting place. Other demons lived there, not old Master."

"And you can't tell me where he lives?"

Dahael answered. "Don't even know anymore. Not same place he lived before."

"Demon moves a lot," Bashiok added.

"Afraid of Mistress and demon skin," Dahael said, nodding.

"Shouldn't you not be able to say that?" I asked, looking at her.

"Mistress knew it already," she said.

I nodded. I hated this enchantment on the imps. My life would have been so much easier if they could just tell me everything they knew. But I also knew that the enchantment kept my friends and I safe, and it safeguarded the imps' lives, as well.

I took a breath, tried to fight back the exhaustion and general feeling that all I wanted to do was hide under my blankets and wait for the storm to pass. "I need to figure out how to do this," I said to them.

"Mistress is not alone. Has team. Has demon skin."

"I don't want anyone else to die because of Astaroth," I said.

Dahael walked closer to me, pulled gently on my pant leg. "Don't blame yourself. Mistress can't control everything, no matter how powerful."

I took another deep breath, looked past the imps at the brick church behind them.

Bashiok cleared his throat. "Mistress. More news."

I crouched down, better able to look at him. I hated

standing above the imps, looking down on them. "What is it?"

"Traitor on demon skin's team."

A chill went down my spine. I knew what he would say before he said it. "Invisible man."

"George," I said, shaking my head.

Bashiok and Dahael nodded. Dahael patted my shoulder.

"For how long?"

"Don't know. But he was at the demon house last night. Heard him talking to demons about you and demon skin."

I sighed. "Crap." I crouched there a moment longer, savoring the momentary calm. Late morning near downtown meant lots of traffic noises and not much else. A symphony of engines, car stereos, and horns. Life went on around us, no matter who died, no matter who betrayed you. Life went on, unknowing, blissfully unaware that nothing more than a reformed demon and a confused mindflayer stood between them and living nightmares that would come to devour them in their sleep.

What would it be like, to feel that way? To go about your everyday life not knowing about the real dangers that existed? So many in this city really struggled with basic life or death things like keeping food on the table, keeping their families safe and whole. They knew dangers. They knew hopelessness. But so many others worried about nothing more than the next new thing, the candy-coated artifice of life.

Those would be the ones most easily targeted by Astaroth and his pals if Nain and I failed. The shifters had made it clear: Astaroth had promised them more. No hiding. No cowering. All they had to do was destroy me.

I would have laughed at the idea that screwed up, antisocial little me was keeping anyone from doing anything, if I wasn't so terrified of messing this up.

There was so much more to the story than this. It

didn't make sense. Astaroth could have made his move any time before I came on the scene. Nain had been cursed, losing his demonic form in the late 1970s. I wasn't even born until 1987, didn't discover most of my powers until a few months ago, when I'd met Nain. So why now? Why was it so vital for Astaroth to take me out now?

We were missing something. Something big.

"Mistress?" Bashiok said, shaking me from the circles I was running in my head.

"Yeah?"

"Puppeteer was there, too."

"We figured they were in cahoots," I said, rubbing my face.

"She talked to invisible man. Planning something, we think."

"Yeah. I'm thinking you're right about that. Let's go." I got in the car, and Bashiok and Dahael climbed in, settling themselves in the back seat. I turned the volume up on the stereo, letting AC/DC give me a sense of kickass I was not feeling at the moment.

Every little bit helped.

We zipped through downtown, and I parked in the garage below Nain's building. Imps greeted us, joined us as I headed onto the elevator.

"Is George here?" I asked one of the imps who'd been standing guard at the building.

"Yes, Mistress. Whole team is here now," he said in a low, gravelly voice. I nodded.

"I want you to stand by," I said, addressing the group of imps. "If he goes invisible, try to keep an eye out for him. I don't want him getting out of the building until Nain decides how to deal with this."

They nodded, thumped their fists to their chests, once. A sign of respect I really didn't deserve. I took a deep breath as the elevator creaked to a stop, and I opened the metal grate, letting the imps and I into the foyer. I used my key to unlock the door and we headed in.

I glanced around the loft. Brennan and Stone sat in the living room, watching baseball. Ada and Nain were in the dining room, looking over some maps Ada had spread on the table. George sat on the steps that led up to his room. I filtered out the others and focused on him, while heading over to where Nain and Ada were. Nain greeted me with a quick hug, then went back to talking to Ada.

George. Nervous, angry. Lots of hatred, especially once he'd noticed me enter the loft. Loss. I tried to get into his head, softly, carefully, in a way he wouldn't notice. His shield was strong. Nain had taught him well.

Nain and Ada finished up, and Nain turned to me. I met his eyes.

We have a traitor, Nain, I thought at him. This would hurt him. So close after Veronica's loss, he would have to deal with George's treachery. He'd taken George in when he was fifteen, homeless, lost, screwed up because of his powers. He'd given George a home and a makeshift family. Made him a force to be reckoned with. And this was how the little shithead repaid him? I was furious on Nain's behalf.

I felt surprise from Nain. Sadness. *George.*

Yeah. The imps saw him hanging out with the Puppeteer at Astaroth's little get together last night. I'm sorry.

He was silent for several moments. Sadness, uncertainty. Then, he finally nodded. He met my eyes one more time, then leaned down and kissed me, just a light brushing of lips against lips.

He walked into the kitchen, which was near where George was sitting. I stayed put, but glanced around the room. The imps had arranged themselves perfectly. Out of the way, but able to see what was going on. Brennan had noticed too, glanced over at me and raised his eyebrows. What's going on? he mouthed at me.

I gave a barely perceptible nod toward Nain and George. Brennan glanced that way, then stood up and strolled toward where Nain was.

I was glad. I knew how hard this was going to be for Nain. While he'd raised Brennan as his son, and the two had grown to become friends (even if they were friends who rarely agreed on anything) he'd done almost the same for George. Brennan and George were the same age, had spent their teenage years hanging out together.

George looked up to see Nain and Brennan watching him.

"What's up?" he asked. I could feel his nervousness spike.

"Did the Puppeteer comfort you well in your time of need, George?" Nain asked. His voice was low, calm. He was doing it again, looking cool and unbothered when his emotions were in turmoil. I hated George a little harder.

George started at Nain in silence. I felt anger from Brennan.

"What are you talking about?" George asked.

"You were seen hanging out with the Puppeteer and other members of Astaroth's crew last night. Care to explain?"

George was silent, glaring at Nain.

"How the hell could you do that, man?" Brennan asked.

Then, George laughed. "Let me guess. Your pet mindflayer told you so. So of course, you believe her. What a joke." Then he laughed again and stood up. "You are pathetic."

"Molly doesn't lie," Brennan said. His offense on my behalf was almost as strong as Nain's.

"And how do you know that? All you know is you're jealous of Nain for getting into her pants first. How do you know she doesn't lie? What do we even know about her, other than she showed up and everything went to shit?"

"Everything was already shit. Or were you not here for all the years we spent fighting backwards assholes, including your pal the Puppeteer?" Brennan asked, his voice still calm, though anger raged through him. He was like Nain in many ways I'd never noticed. This was another of those times.

"Veronica is dead because of her!" George shouted, jabbing a finger toward me. "Or did all of you assholes forget that the whole reason we were there last night was because Astaroth used us to lure her there? Wake the fuck up!" he finished.

I had to remember to breathe against the sick feeling inside me. He wasn't saying anything I hadn't already said. He was right, about that much at least.

"Veronica is dead because a power-hungry shifter used her and a bunch of innocent Normals to gain favor with Astaroth," Nain said. "Why he used them is irrelevant. You want to blame someone for Veronica's death, blame Astaroth. Blame the shifter who slit her throat."

"And since he's the one you should be blaming, hanging out with his people is a really sick way to honor Roni's memory," Brennan added.

The room was silent. Ada and Stone stood in the dining room, watching the group near the stairs. The imps were ready, watching.

"The Puppeteer swears that all he wants is her," George said. "Why should we get involved in this shit?"

"How much did you tell them, George?" Nain asked. Furious.

"I didn't need to tell them anything! They know already. You think they don't know where to find us? They don't care. You're not a threat to Astaroth anymore, Nain. He wants her," he said, waving at me again. "They know where she lives, where we live. They know you two are sleeping together. They know everything. They're just waiting for their chance."

"Why were you with them?" Nain asked.

"Because I'm with them on this. She's not worth any of this shit. She's not worth losing Veronica."

I had to respect him. He was a dickhead, and he was stupid for getting pulled into Astaroth's clutches, but he stood there in front of a very pissed off demon and an equally pissed shapeshifter, and told not just them, but me (someone who scared the living shit out of him) exactly what he thought of me. It took guts, or cluelessness. George was many things, but he wasn't clueless.

Let him go, I thought to Nain. *What else can you do?*

I can't just let him go. What kind of message does that send? Double-cross me, and go on your merry way? That doesn't work.

You can't kill him.

A few seconds of nothing, while Nain sized up George. George stood, staring back at him. His hands shook, but he was doing a very good job of keeping a rein on the fear inside of him. Resignation that it was over, that he was finished.

I can't kill him. But you can erase his memory.

No.

George laughed then. "Working it all out with your enforcer, Nain? Just finish me. I'll even make it easy for you." He spread his arms and stood, ready. Terrified, but ready.

Molly, do it. Nain thought at me, the command unmistakable in his tone.

Don't do that, I warned. *I'm not doing it. Take his memory, then what? Leave him helpless against the world? No.*

I sensed anger from Nain. At me. At George, at everything.

Just let him go.

Nain growled. Closed his mind off from me, something he'd never done before. It was like having a door slammed in my face. "Pack. Leave. Don't let me see you again. You have ten minutes."

Then he stalked out of the loft without looking at me, slamming the door behind him.

I spent most of the rest of the day with Ada. She was determined to either teach me a spell or two to protect myself, or craft an object or two to help shield me from magical attacks like the one that had taken Nain's demonic form from him.

We tried simple conjurings; a spell that would shield me from flames. I tried, over and over again, and never felt anything like the buzzing that Ada described as the calm before the storm; those moments before a spell takes hold. After my sixth try, I threw my hands up in frustration.

"This is impossible!" I said, flopping down onto the wood floor in the training area. Ada laughed. Brennan was sitting, watching us, leaning against the wall.

"It's okay, honey," Ada said, coming and sitting down next to me. "I figured it wouldn't work. Demons usually aren't able to work even the simplest of spells. But I figured with that little spark of something else in you, maybe you'd be able to. I'll make you an amulet instead."

"Thanks. Would have been a useful thing to learn," I said, irritated with myself.

"You can't be good at everything, Molly," Brennan said.

"Yeah. Leave some talent for the rest of us," Ada joked, nudging me with her elbow. The she got serious. "The only bad thing about an amulet or other item like that is that you have to make sure it's on you at all times. Astaroth has witches. Why he hasn't tried something like what he did to Nain against you already is a mystery."

"He wants her powers," Brennan said. "He wanted Nain dead. He wants her alive."

"Thank you for that cheerful interjection, Bren," I said, standing up and pulling Ada with me. The two of us walked into the kitchen, and Brennan followed. Ada grabbed a cup of coffee and headed into her room/lab to start working on my amulet. Brennan and I stayed in the kitchen, scrounging through the cabinets for something to eat.

"Someone needs to hit the grocery store," Brennan grumbled.

"It's your week, isn't it?"

"Shut up, Molly," he said, laughing. "You were supposed to volunteer."

"Grocery shopping is another talent I lack. The one time Veronica came over, all I had to give her was cold cereal. I was just grateful the milk wasn't expired." Mentioning Veronica ended the moment of levity. We'd lost so much. I didn't think I could stand to lose anymore.

"What happened with George?" Brennan asked, studying my face. "I know you and Nain were doing your creepy telepath thing. Nain was pissed when he left here. What happened?"

I resumed my futile search for something salty and bad for me. Stone ate all the good stuff as soon as it came into the loft. "We had a disagreement," I finally said.

"Yeah, duh. About what?" he asked, leaning against the counter and crossing his arms.

I almost told him. Confided in him. I wanted to. I wanted someone to make me feel like less of an idiot for the way I'd reacted with George. And Brennan would have. He would have understood why what Nain had demanded of me, erasing George's memory, was wrong.

But this was between Nain and I. Bringing someone else into it, especially Brennan, was wrong, too. I just shook my head.

We were silent for a few minutes, standing there in the kitchen. Frustration rolled off of him. "Well, let me guess," he said. "He wanted you to use your powers to do something to George that would both punish him and minimize him as a threat. He wanted you to do whatever because he couldn't kill George, no matter how often he threatens to do it if one of us ever poses a threat to the others. And you said no." He met my eyes. "You don't even have to say anything. I know enough about how Nain works to guess why he's pissed off at you right now."

He came closer to me, took my hand, the one that now sported Nain's ring.

"I guess congratulations are in order. I noticed his earlier, before he stormed out."

I pulled my hand back and glanced up at him. Brennan sighed. "Just, don't lose yourself in this, Molly. You're good. You're so good, and you don't even realize it. You're a nightmare. Terrifying. But there's something in you that shines. Don't lose that. Even when you have to be a nightmare. Even when you have to make your enemies tremble before you. Don't lose yourself."

"I am trying not to," I said, turning and walking out of the loft. Bashiok and Dahael were stationed in the foyer, as always.

"The house. Any idea if any of them are still there?" I asked, digging through my pockets, seeing what I had on me. Knife. Pepper spray. Phone. It was good enough.

"Yes, Mistress. Demons stayed. Not old master, but the other ones. Lower demons," Bashiok said, a note of obvious dislike in his voice.

"Any idea how many?"

"At least six."

I nodded. Pressed the elevator button and stood, waiting. Felt Brennan behind me before he even opened the door and stepped into the foyer with us.

"Wherever you're going, can I come? I assume there's going to be asskicking involved," he said.

I glanced at him. "It's probably better if I go myself." Bashiok shook his head in disbelief, staring at me.

Brennan laughed. "I don't think Bash agrees," he said. I glared at both of them. "Come on, Molly. I need to do something with all of this shit I'm feeling."

The elevator creaked to a halt, and I opened the door, waving Brennan inside. "Fine. Let's go destroy some demons, then."

He grinned. "Excellent."

CHAPTER FOURTEEN

We sped to the neighborhood Bash and Dahael directed me to, radio cranked up, Brennan in the passenger seat nodding along to the beat, six imps sitting in the back seat like small, terrifying children. Even the imps seemed to have some fight in them today. I had kept them on a short leash since they'd pledged themselves to me. No more rampaging, not more causing trouble, no more instigating fights between the Normals. I met Bashiok's gaze in the rear view mirror. "Do you want in on this?" I asked him, shouting above the stereo.

"It would be an honor, Mistress," he said, baring his sharp little teeth in a terrifying grin. The other imps nodded in agreement. I could feel excitement from them. The crazy little bastards were actually looking forward to fighting demons.

They weren't the only ones.

I didn't make a secret of our presence when we pulled up to the brick ranch. Radio blaring, tires squealing as I braked at the curb. I jammed the car into park, and Brennan and the imps followed me as I stalked toward the house.

And when the Puppeteer walked out onto the front

porch, I couldn't stop myself from giving her what I hoped was a disturbing, creepy smile. Yeah. This was going to make me feel a whole lot better.

At least, that was what I thought, until I heard Brennan groaning behind me, and the Puppeteer's bubbly, childlike laugh.

I turned to glance at Brennan to see him holding his head in his hands. Then I felt the Puppeteer's presence, trying to poke her way into my mind.

I'd been preparing for this, of course. All of that work with Nain, all of the migraines, all of the practice, even as I drifted off to sleep at night– all of it had been because I never wanted to feel her slimy presence in my mind again.

And it was worth it. It took no effort to keep her out. I turned back to her as I felt annoyance start rolling off of her.

"My, we've gotten stronger, haven't we?" she finally said in her annoying, saccharine voice. I just glared at her. Brennan groaned again behind me.

"Unfortunately for you, I can't say the same for him." She smiled at me, and I lunged for her.

"Grab her," the Puppeteer barked, and Brennan grabbed my arms from behind, holding me in a vise-like grip as I tried to lunge for her again. "Just hold her, puppet," the Puppeteer said as if she was speaking to a dog; smiling again. I struggled against Brennan's grip, but it was pointless.

The Puppeteer closed her eyes. "Oh, this is too easy. I wonder if you have any idea how tumultuous his thoughts are regarding you." She opened her eyes, winked at me, closed them again. "Desire. He wants you, more than he's ever wanted anything. The fantasies he has about you! He's pretty sure he loves you. Silly boy," she said, giggling. "Falling in love with a demon is a terrible idea."

I struggled against Brennan again. Useless. I tried to feel for anyone else around. No supernatural presences, other than the three of us and the imps, who had flanked me, waiting for my command.

"But, there's so much more. Anger. He feels betrayed by you. He wonders why he's not good enough for you. You make him feel worthless, and this is something a shapeshifter can't abide. They are a proud race, shifters. And you have turned him away, over and over again. Part of him hates you."

I went still, her words doing more damage to me than I wanted to let on. Brennan was silent behind me, his hands on my arms. I could feel my biceps bruising under his grip.

"Isn't that right, puppet?" The Puppeteer said to Brennan.

"Yes, my Lady," he said, his voice a monotone.

"I can use that. All of it," the Puppeteer murmured, looking at me again in that creepy way she had. "I nearly ran, when I saw your car. I can admit that. Astaroth had just left me. We don't get much alone time anymore, thanks to you." She pouted, for just a moment. "I know you're stronger than I am in some ways, dear. But I thought you'd be smarter. I thought you'd come alone, or that you'd bring your pet demon with you. But you brought me a gift instead." And she giggled again, and my stomach turned.

"Puppet, see that she is disabled. I want her weak, unconscious. I owe Astaroth an anniversary gift. She'll do nicely."

And that was when Brennan's hands went from my arms to my throat, and he started choking me from behind, strong fingers digging into my windpipe.

I thrashed my head back, heard a wet sound as his nose broke. His grip loosened, and I leapt away.

"Sorry, Bren," I said to the man I hoped was still inside there somewhere.

He lunged for me again, and I did all I could to evade. I dodged, I ducked, I ran. I didn't want to get too far away from the Puppeteer. I had to be close to her if I wanted to kill her.

And I did. Oh, I did. I would.

"Do whatever it takes," the Puppeteer said. "I know this much about the Angel," she said, with a note of disdain in her voice, "she won't hurt one of the few people who have ever cared about her. Weakness. Keep her alive. Barely." And with that, she sat down on one of the white plastic chairs on the porch, crossed her legs, and watched us with a look on her face that reminded me of a child at the circus.

God, I hated her.

Brennan kept lunging for me. He shifted into a cat. His animal forms were always harder to fight. They were stronger, faster, than his human form. And they had sharp teeth and claws. I twisted away, just missing being raked across the stomach by his claws.

"Brennan, remember me," I murmured. I knew trying to mess around in his mind was pointless. I'd already seen what happened when I tried to cut the connection to the Puppeteer. Her puppets ended up very much dead.

"Remember," I said again. I may as well have been talking to a statue. He slashed at me again, catching my thigh. I grunted as I felt claws slice through muscle.

"Imps!" I pointed at the Puppeteer, and my six imps charged.

"Oh, please," she said. "Sleep!" she ordered my imps, and they fell to the ground, snoring.

"Don't order my imps around, you bitch," I growled, evading another swipe from Brennan's claws. I started focusing on the Puppeteer. Well, as much as I could while trying to avoid being sliced to ribbons by Brennan. I was losing blood quickly. If I was going to do this, it had to be now, when I still had most of my power available to me. Before he damaged my body much more.

I evaded snapping jaws aimed for my throat, kicked panther-Brennan across the front yard.

She was right. I wouldn't hurt Brennan more than I absolutely had to.

The only thing I could do was focus on her, ending her.

I started poking at her mind. She felt me immediately, and I felt panic from her. "Faster, you idiot!" she yelled at Brennan.

I continued hammering at her mind, trying to break past her defenses. Her shield was strong. Stronger than Nain's, even. Where my shield was a steel box, hers was a sphere; smooth, metallic. No weak points.

I kept working at her.

This takes focus, which is a problem when you're supposed to be fighting for your life. I missed it when Brennan lunged for me again, and his claws sliced my abdomen open.

The Puppeteer cheered. Smug bitch.

I could feel my power lessening as I required more energy for healing myself.

I started to shiver. Too much blood loss.

I'd die before I'd let her take me to Astaroth. No way.

I kept working at her mind. This was pointless. She laughed at me. Her confidence soared in the face of my weakening power.

"Poor baby," she cooed. "I can't imagine why anyone wants you this much. You're really not anything special."

"Your boyfriend wants me pretty bad," I said, darting away from Brennan again. I felt a spike of annoyance from her.

"Oh, please. He doesn't want you. He's promised you to someone else. He was perfectly happy avoiding that demon and his team. He only came out of hiding because he had to."

This wasn't working. The Puppeteer was crazy. She was vile. But she was a stronger telepath than I was. I was barely standing. Fighting Brennan, healing from the injuries he was giving me, was taking everything I had.

I did the only thing I knew she was really afraid of. I ran toward her.

She jumped up out of her chair, tripped over the

sleeping imps as she tried to run off of the porch, away from me.

"Get her!" she shrieked as I advanced on her.

Brennan had shifted back into his human form again, ran for me as I reached the Puppeteer. I punched her in the face, hard. She crumpled into a whimpering ball on the porch.

That was for me, and it felt good.

I drew my fist back again. I grabbed the front of her shirt and got ready to punch again.

And that was when Brennan kicked my leg, from the side.

I heard a crack, and warm blood dripped down my leg as the pain became unbearable. I was dizzy with it. I glanced down to see my femur poking out of the side of my jeans, jagged edge cutting right through the denim.

I fell down, still gripping the front of the Puppeteer's shirt. She laughed.

If I did nothing else in this life, I was going to destroy her. With every ounce of power I had left, I grabbed her head.

And twisted, hard. Fast. I put every ounce of hatred and anger I was feeling into it.

I heard a satisfying snap, felt her presence fade. I rolled off of her, and the movement jostled my broken leg. The pain was too much, and my world faded to black.

I don't think I was out very long. I felt gentle hands washing blood away from my stomach, arms. I opened my eyes to see Dahael handing Bashiok one bloody washcloth as he handed her a clean one. Teamwork.

Blood was still flowing from my stomach and leg. An imp was holding a towel over the rip in my abdomen, trying to staunch the bleeding. I glanced around. It was still early evening, and the cicadas buzzed in the trees. I looked to my left to see the Puppeteer's body. I tried to sit up, remembering.

Two of the other imps pushed me back down, gently.

"Must heal, Mistress," one of them said apologetically.

"Brennan," I said, barely able to form the word. My mouth was dry, and my throat was swollen. Everything hurt.

"Alive. Unconscious," Dahael said softly. "Be still."

I did. My leg was not healing yet. The gashes on my stomach were closing. My throat was less painful. Cuts across my arms and hips were already gone. But the bone sticking out of my thigh was going to be a problem.

I heard a groan, and glanced toward where Brennan was. He sat up, slowly, rubbing his head. I was so relieved I could have cried. Later.

He looked around and his gaze landed on me, surrounded by my imps. He jumped up, ran toward me. He reached out to take my hand.

I flinched away from him, before I even realized what I was doing.

I felt shame flood from him. And then he looked over my body, saw my thigh.

He turned away from me, and I heard him vomiting over the side of the porch. Anger, shame, helplessness flooded from him. Disgust.

He retched a few more times. Bashiok handed him a towel, and he wiped at his face with it. He stayed that way, facing away from me.

"Brennan. I need your help," I said, ignoring the fear that rose up at even the idea of having him touch me again.

He turned to me then. His eyes were haunted, his face gaunt. "What can I do?"

"If we don't get this leg straightened up, it's never going to be right again," I said, and I felt fear grip him. "I need you to help me. I can't do it alone."

"The imps—"

"Are not strong enough. I need you to do this for me."

"Nain…" he said.

"He won't get here soon enough. Oh, fuck it. I'll do it

myself." I waved him off, started trying to pull at my knee to give myself room to maneuver the bone back toward where it was supposed to be. Pain exploded, and I was on the verge of puking.

"Stop it. Stop. I'll help," he said. He came to me. "Tell me what to do."

"Pull, at the knee. Toward you. Dahael, push the bone back in when there's room," I said, grabbing my thigh just above where it was broken.

"On three."

"Shit," Brennan groaned.

"One. Two. Three," I said, and we all pulled and pushed at the same time.

I screamed as Brennan tugged on my leg. I felt Dahael shove the sharp, broken bone back into place, felt every movement in agonizing detail as she lined it back up.

"Release," she said once the bone was back in place.

Brennan and I both let go of our respective parts of my leg. He staggered away and puked again. I laid back on the porch and just tried to stay conscious. I was sweating, and shivering, and hyperventilating…something I'd never done in my life.

Dahael came back to me, put a cool washcloth on my forehead. "Deep breaths, Mistress," she said softly, her voice warm. "Calm. Calm." I tried to force my breathing to slow, felt even weaker as tears came to my eyes, and I couldn't fight them back.

"Calm, Mistress. Victorious. So strong, Mistress," Bashiok said, kneeling next to Dahael and patting my shoulder with his knobby little hand.

I tried. I tried not to think. I focused on my body, healing itself. At the fire in my thigh as bone, muscle, skin fused itself back together again.

Dahael lifted the towel off of my stomach. "Healed," she said, nodding in approval.

"I'm going to call Nain," Brennan said. "He should come and take you home."

"No," I said. He stopped reaching for his phone, looked at me. "I can't deal with his reaction right now. You know how he is."

I felt shame, helplessness flow from him. "I need to get out of here, Molly. I am so sorry. I nearly killed you, and you're afraid of me now and I can't even—"

"Brennan. That was the Puppeteer," I said softly. No point in denying that I was afraid of him. I'd never felt the full impact of Brennan's strength. I'd always felt safe around him, knowing he'd protect me to the death if he had to. I wanted that back. But all I could see right then was the look of sheer hatred he'd had on his face when he advanced on me, ready to kill.

"I could see and hear everything," he said, so softly I barely heard it. "She was in control, but I watched, like I was watching a TV show, helpless to change what was going on. I heard everything she said. I felt my claws slice through your skin. I listened to you beg me, listened to you scream. I heard her tell you every thought I've had about you. She used me as her own personal thug. I don't even want to be around me now. I can only imagine what you feel."

I was silent. He stood there, not looking at me. "Bren. This is all about to come to an end. It has to. We need you. Once this is over, take all the time you need. I plan on doing the same. But we need you. I need your help," I said, words that had never left my lips before. "We've already lost so much."

He finally looked at me, then. Nodded. "Loft, or your house?"

"My house. I can get changed and cleaned up there." He helped me stand up, and I tried again not to recoil from his touch. We paused for a moment while I waited for the dizziness to pass. "I think this is one of those things Nain doesn't need to know about," I said after a while, as we started to walk toward my car.

"You're going to lie to him?" he asked, supporting me

as I dug through my pockets for my car keys.

"I'll tell him we fought the Puppeteer and won. He doesn't need to know the details." I could only imagine how he'd come down on Brennan then. I could feel how he was feeling. He hated himself enough without Nain adding to it.

I looked up to see Brennan staring at me, eyes still haunted. "Are you sure?"

"There's plenty he keeps from me, believe me," I said, getting in on the passenger side and handing him my keys. He helped me swing my injured leg into the car and closed the door. I breathed against the panic that tried to set in as he got into the car with me and closed his door. I closed my eyes, forced tears back again. This was not the time to fall apart.

Maybe later.

Brennan and I didn't exchange a single word on the way to my house. I gripped the passenger side door as he drove, fast, but still carefully, through the neighborhoods. I rolled my window down, just tried to remember to breathe.

My leg still ached. I wondered if we'd managed to get it back together right. Dahael had done the best she could, but sticking ones' hands into a gaping wound to try to set a bone is hardly a surgical-quality repair. All I knew was, it hurt.

The imps sat in the back seat. Silent. I glanced over at Brennan. His hands gripped the steering wheel. His knuckles were white. I didn't have to be able to read emotions to know how he was feeling right then. His face was pale, jaw set. His easy grin was nowhere in sight now.

I looked away, watched houses and trees blur as we zipped past them.

When we got to my house, he jumped out of the car and jogged over to my side to help me. I was already up and out.

"It's okay. I've got it," I said, trying not to visibly recoil from him again. I started walking toward the house, limping on my bad leg. It had stopped bleeding, and the skin had healed itself. The rest would take a while. Brennan walked behind me, ready to catch me if I fell. He kept his hands away from me, though, and I was grateful for it.

He followed me into the house and up the stairs.

"I'll be outside," he said once I was in my room. Then he turned and left without another word.

I ran a hot bath and settled into it, lowering myself gingerly into the old-fashioned claw foot tub. The water was almost too hot. The heat soothed my aching body, made me feel a little less disgusting.

I ran a sponge over my body, dunked my head under the water and washed my hair. Then I settled back and closed my eyes.

I was just drifting off when I felt Nain's presence nearby, then, sure enough, heavy footsteps on the stairs. I sensed for Brennan. Gone, far enough away that I couldn't feel him anymore.

Nain knocked at the door. "Molly?"

"Come on in." I glanced at the tub. Bubbles still covered the surface of the water. It shouldn't have mattered. The man had seen every inch of my body. But right then, I couldn't stand the idea of being seen.

The door opened, and he came in, filling my small bathroom with his body, his power. He glanced at me, then knelt next to the tub, picked up the sponge from the small tray across the tub. "Want me to do your back?" he asked.

I nodded, sat forward enough so he could get to my back. He dipped the sponge in the hot water, started to gently scrub my back.

"Brennan couldn't get out of here fast enough," he finally said, rubbing the sponge over my shoulders. I let my head hang forward, and he washed the back of my neck.

"Did he say anything to you?" I asked.

"Only that I should take care of you," he said.

We were quiet for a while. "We fought the Puppeteer," I finally said. "We won."

His hand stopped. Surprise, concern. "You should both be really happy, then. She was a big piece of the puzzle. You both look like someone just died."

I shrugged. "It was a hard fight. We almost didn't win."

"You were in a lot of pain. It was crippling," he said. I'd forgotten that he could feel me through our marriage bond now.

"Yeah. It was rough," I said, not knowing what else to say. He went back to washing my back, slow, methodical strokes. "Did you know she was screwing Astaroth?"

"Yeah. They've been together for a really long time."

"And you didn't think that was worth sharing with me?"

"Why did you two come here? Why didn't you come back to the loft when you were done?"

"You didn't answer my question. Again," I said.

"Answer mine first."

"We came here because I was out of clothes again and I was gross and wanted to get cleaned up. He stayed because you two both seem to think I need someone watching my back all the time. Satisfied?"

"Not really. He looked guilty about something. And you are nervous. There's something you're not telling me."

"Join the club," I muttered, shoving his hand away from my shoulder.

He stood up and rubbed his hands over his face. "I'm not going to tell you everything. You know that. I have my reasons."

"And I'm just supposed to be okay with that?"

"It's the way it is. I tell you what you need to know."

I stared at him. "Are you serious? We did this goddamned marriage bond thing and you still can't be straight with me?"

"Did you think marrying me would change me?" He

laughed. "Come on, little girl. You know me better than that."

"If….fine. Forget it." I'd almost said it. Almost let a whiny "if you really loved me…" escape my lips. I was tired. I was still freaking out over what I'd just been through. I felt weak. That had to be it.

"I love you. You know I do."

"Why didn't you tell me about Astaroth and the Puppeteer?"

He growled, looked up at the ceiling in irritation. "Because I really didn't think it mattered. Did it?"

"It kind of did. She was going to give me to him as an anniversary present."

"So? The vampire wanted to give you to Astaroth, too, and they weren't sleeping together. At least, I don't think they were." He shrugged.

"Astaroth isn't the one who wants me, though," I said.

Nain stilled. "What are you talking about?"

"The Puppeteer said he's basically just the headhunter. Someone else wants me, and it's Astaroth's job to bring me in."

"That can't be right. Astaroth's no one's errand boy," he said, shaking his head.

"Why else would she say it, then?"

"I don't know. Maybe because she's a crazy bitch?"

"Maybe Astaroth lied to her. Maybe it's a demon thing," I said, standing up and grabbing a towel off of the towel bar. I wrapped it around my body and stalked toward my room. My leg still hurt, but at least I wasn't limping.

"Maybe she can't follow simple orders and he's not entirely sure he can trust her," he shouted at me as I slammed my bedroom door.

"Just leave, Nain," I shouted back at him. "This is the last thing I need right now."

"Right. Should I have Brenny-poo come back?" he roared.

"How about you both just stay away?" I screeched at him. The house groaned and creaked around me. My power was at a fever pitch.

I heard his footsteps as he headed down the stairs, heard him slam the back door. A few seconds later, he gunned the truck's engine and roared off down the street.

CHAPTER FIFTEEN

I threw on a pair of soft pajama pants and a tank top and crawled between my soft, cool cotton sheets. Turned the light out and laid there. Sleep wouldn't come. I watched the shadows of tree branches dance across my walls. I could hear the imps downstairs, watching Letterman, then some crappy late night movie. They seemed to like hokey old horror movies. Twilight Zone was a big hit, too.

I heard Nain's truck pull into the driveway a little after two. He walked in and climbed the stairs.

He opened the bedroom door, and I heard him rustling around, removing shoes, clothing. He climbed into bed next to me, and pulled me into his arms. Part of me wanted to melt against him, take the strength and warmth I so badly needed. Part of me was furious with him for all of the shit that had happened that day. For not trusting me. For not being what I needed him to be.

We laid there in silence for a long time, his body cocooning mine, his scent surrounding me.

"I don't want to fight with you, Molly," he murmured against my hair as he buried his face into it. "I love you. I trust you. I'm sorry I'm an asshole. Believe it or not, I am trying not to be."

I felt tears sting my eyes. I felt myself strengthening, felt more alive just from being near him. Partly because of the weird connection we had, the way he could feed me with his ever-present anger. But mostly because I loved him. He infuriated me. He made me crazy. All I knew was that things seemed less nightmarish with him at my side.

I ran my fingertips over his forearms, and he held me tighter, as if he couldn't get close enough.

"This will all be over soon," he said after a while.

"And then we get our happily ever after," I said. I felt my eyelids getting heavy. "We should find a nice little secluded cabin in the woods. Somewhere with a little lake nearby. We can skinny dip whenever we want, and fall asleep in front of a roaring fire. And we can just stay there forever." I yawned, and he kissed my shoulder.

"That sounds as close to heaven as I'm ever going to get," Nain said.

I smiled and finally drifted off to sleep.

When I woke up, I was alone in bed. But I smelled coffee and bacon, and I heard the oldies station playing on the kitchen radio. Nain had an affinity for Motown stuff from the 50s and 60s. I smiled. Couldn't fault his taste in music.

I got up, dressed in jeans and a long sleeved black top. I brushed my hair out, but left it down. I wanted to feel Nain's fingers running through it, and I knew I would. He couldn't resist doing that.

I was strong, strengthened from spending the night next to him, feeding and healing. My leg was a little sore still, but I was sure now that it would heal completely. I tried not to think about how it had happened. I'd had one nightmare about it the night before, a dream in which Brennan came after me again and again, broke so many bones that I was unable to move at all anymore. I woke with a start as he transformed into a bear and was about to tear into my throat. Nain had pulled me closer to him, murmured that it was okay, he was there, and we'd both drifted back off to sleep.

I went downstairs, strolled into the kitchen. He was plating up bacon and eggs, toast. He smiled at me when he saw me, and I walked over and kissed him, slow and soft. Desire flooded him, me. I bit his lower lip, gently, before drawing away, and felt a spike of need from him.

"You like it when I bite you," I said, laughing.

He groaned a little, tweaked my hip as I walked past him. I sat down and he placed a plate in front of me, poured a cup of coffee and added plenty of cream and sugar, just the way I liked it. We sat down and ate in companionable silence, listening to the morning DJs banter with each other between music by the Four Tops and the Jackson 5. I sensed for him. He was tense, as always. Undercurrent of rage that was just Nain, even when he was happy. Demon. Nervous. A little sad.

I glanced up at him. "How are you holding up?"

He shook his head. "I still can't really believe she's gone. She came to me when she was fifteen, scrawny little kid terrified of herself. Ada was thrilled to have a girl to raise, finally. And then George came to me, and they were inseparable. I can't believe George…" he shook his head again. "I never knew losing someone was this hard. I don't think I really was able to feel a lot of this shit until you came into my life."

"We seem to have changed each other quite a bit, then," I said, meeting his eyes.

He was silent for a while. Then, "I think we should do the marriage ritual again."

I raised my eyebrow. "Once was not enough?"

"It was. But I want… I want to feel more of you in me." He swallowed, and I got a sense from him. Mourning.

"You're thinking of George and Veronica again."

He didn't answer.

I stood up, pulled up my sleeve. I grabbed one of my knives from the counter. Then I rifled through the old first aid kit I kept under the sink, came up with an ace bandage.

I walked over to Nain, nudged him, and he pushed his chair back from the table. Once we had room, I straddled his lap, sat down and felt his legs, strong and solid under mine. I met his eyes, slashed my right wrist in one quick movement. He did the same, and we joined the wounds together, just as we had on our wedding night. We wrapped our wrists, sat there, rested our foreheads against each other. I felt his blood flow into me, and contentment flowed through him as my blood entered his body. Shivers went up my spine.

Our hearts beat in unison. His blood, his emotions coursed through me. His thoughts were an open book, and every thought he had was for me, how much he loved me, needed me. How afraid he was of losing me. He belonged to me, entirely, in that moment.

Do you feel that? You can feel, you can hear, how much I love you.

I nodded, my forehead still resting against his. Tears stung my eyes.

Know how much I love you, Molly. Know that I would never intentionally hurt you. Know that I am going to ask you to do things that you're going to hate me for. I ask them because I don't have any other choice.

Tell me.

This is ending. We both know it's only a matter of time. You killed his lover, his mate. He bonded to her, just as you are to me. He will not let that go. He may have promised you to someone else, but he'll be after blood now. He's in mourning. Imagine what it would feel like to have this bond broken.

That will never happen.

Well. Imagine how you would feel. He's feeling that. You'd want to destroy anyone who broke our bond, wouldn't you?

I nodded.

He won't wait any more. He won't be hiding. He will come after you with everything he has. You need to destroy him.

I am stronger than him.

But he is more skilled. He knows tricks you haven't even thought of. Brute force will be necessary to take him out. It's your only chance.

I have that.

I felt humor from him. *Molly smash.*

We just sat, absorbing each other, for a minute. He continued. *You'll need more. You need to be so powerful he won't stand a chance. And you know how to become more powerful.*

Mind flaying.

I know you hate it. I know you don't want to use those powers. But you need to do this, baby. He'll always be surrounded by others with power. It's how he is. Makes him feel like some kind of little king to have an entourage of the powerful. Use them. Take everything you can. Make yourself fucking invincible.

I felt sick, but I nodded.

And when I give the order, take him out. Don't second-guess me. Don't hesitate. Just do what I tell you to do.

Is this why you got so pissed off with me over that whole George thing?

I need to know that you'll take an order when it matters. I am sorry I did that to you. It was wrong, and I'm glad you put me in my place. But this time, I need to know you'll do what I tell you to do. Just this once.

I didn't answer for a minute. Our wounds had closed, his blood racing through my veins. *I promise. Just this once, Bael.*

I felt relief flood through him. Then he kissed me, long, slow, gently. We held hands, fingers entwined.

I heard the Supremes' "Someday We'll Be Together" start playing on the radio.

"Dance with me, Molly," he murmured against my lips. I nodded, and we stood up, still bound at the wrist. He wrapped his free arm around me, and I rested my cheek against his chest. I listened to his heart beat, strong and steady; felt his chest rise and fall with each breath he took. Reveled in the sensation of his blood flowing even more strongly through my body. We swayed, barely moving, not at all in tempo with the music. It didn't matter. The morning sun streamed in through the kitchen window, and I felt warm, safe, and loved. I could have stayed that way forever with him. His fingers tangled lazily in the ends of my hair, and I smiled against him.

The song ended, and Bashiok and Dahael appeared in the doorway. "Mistress, demon. Lower demon was here. Left a package." His face twisted in disgust as he handed over a cardboard box.

Ashes. With a note.

"You can have Georgie boy back now. You're next."

Nain and I looked at each other. I felt his rage and guilt wash over me. "It would have been better for him if you'd done what I wanted you to do," he said.

"Don't even. Let's not do this again," I said.

He took a deep breath. Dahael and Bash had retreated after they'd delivered the package, and we were alone again. The kitchen, which had seemed so warm and safe just moments before, felt empty now. My stomach churned with anger, guilt. I'd never liked George, but he didn't deserve the terrible end he'd undoubtedly met.

Nain held the box of George's ashes in his hands. I held the note. He was about to say something, when I felt the presence of one of the Guardians. It was unmistakable, a tidal wave of power that felt strong enough to knock me over. I'd felt them at Veronica's funeral, and it wasn't a sensation that was easily forgotten. Within seconds, she seemed to appear out of nowhere, swooping into the kitchen and landing silently, gracefully, near where Nain and I stood.

It was the same Guardian who had stopped and studied me on that night. While they looked similar to one another, there were differences. This one's hair was curlier, wilder. Her nails were blood-red, instead of black. And, of course, she was the only of the Guardians who deigned to notice the existence of the Earth-bound among us.

She looked up at me with her glowing red eyes, cocked her head to the side. Her glance went to the box Nain was holding.

"His soul has been freed," she said, in a voice that carried the weight of time, yet still sounded innocent, somehow. "My sisters transported him as the sun rose."

I nodded. Nain just stared. "Thank you, Guardian," I murmured, bowing my head toward her, just a little. It seemed like the right thing to do.

"You may call me by my name. I am Eunomia," she said, watching me. Again, I was reminded of a particularly deadly, but beautiful, bird.

"Eunomia," I repeated. "Thank you."

"Evil times, demon girl," she said.

I nodded. "I am hoping to end some of it, very soon."

"Sooner, rather than later," she said. "I am not supposed to interfere. Your friends have been ambushed by the one you hunt. He seeks to draw you out. An army lies in wait. Your imps will appear, momentarily, with the same message."

I stared, dread settling over me. Sure enough, within an instant, two of my imps arrived in the kitchen.

"Mistress. Old master snuck up on wild man, witch, strongman when they were chasing a werewolf pack. Big trouble."

Nain was already pulling his shoes on. I stuffed my knife, the note, into my pockets. "Where?"

"Abandoned factory. Crumbled building," he said.

"The Packard plant," I said to Nain, able to picture what the imp was trying to tell me. He gave me a terse nod.

I glanced at the Guardian. "Thank you."

She nodded, and winked out of sight. Nain and I ran outside, got into my car, and I gunned it toward the area in which the crumbling old factory sat. I drove fast, careening through streets that were, thankfully, mostly empty at this time of morning on a Sunday. My hands gripped the steering wheel, and all I could do was hope that I wouldn't be too late.

"Molly, slow down a little."

"Are you kidding? He could be killing them right goddamned now! Why the hell would they go out like this, without telling us first?"

"They want to feel better. You understand that. Slow down, just a little. I want to exchange blood again."

I glanced at him. "You're thinking of something like this now? We just did this, less than an hour ago? Remember?"

Irritation. "Yes, darling," he said through clenched teeth. "Of course I remember. We should do it again. Now, before we get there."

I shook my head.

"Humor me, Molly."

"I do not believe this," I muttered. I dug in my pocket for my knife, left the cutting and binding to him so I could keep driving. I barely felt it when he sliced my wrist open. Within seconds, we were again bound, wrist to wrist. I slowed down. Focusing completely on driving was nearly impossible.

I wouldn't admit it to him, but it soothed me, feeling his blood flow into me again. "You are making this a habit, Nain," I murmured.

"I've told you that you're addictive," he said, holding our wrists together with his other hand. Our pulses raced, and as his blood flowed into me, I felt connected to him, strengthened. I felt nearly invincible.

"I am so ready to kick some demon ass," I said.

Nain snorted. "My blood is good for that."

I glanced at him. "It is good, period."

He gave me a small smile, and brought my wrist, now healed, to his lips. He pressed his lips to the area he'd sliced open, and I shivered at the sensation.

"I love you," he said quietly. "I don't think you'll ever understand how much."

I tangled my fingers in his as I kept steering through the streets. "I love you, too."

"When we get there, start feeding. Start flaying. Take everything you can, from anyone you can. No mercy. Do not hold back," he said, and his voice was a little hoarse. I glanced over at him. He continued. "I'll feel it when you're filled. When you can't take anymore. I'll keep Astaroth busy until you've reached that point. When you do, when I feel it, I'll make sure he's distracted, and I'll give the order. Destroy him. Do not hesitate. Do not listen to anything he tries to say. Just do what you promised me you'd do."

The factory was just ahead. I stopped the car and turned to him. I brought his hand to my lips, kissed his knuckles. "I promise. I trust you. Trust me to do what I said I would."

"I do," he murmured, leaning over and kissing me, just the barest fluttering of his lips on mine.

"You can do better than that," I said, pulling him closer and pressing my lips to his.

He groaned and kissed me once, firmly. He was nervous, tense. Angry. So angry. "Let's get this over with," he said, pulling away and opening the car door. I followed.

I could feel how much energy was being thrown around in the factory as we approached it. I could feel Brennan there, Ada, Stone. Lots of other beings I didn't want anywhere near my friends.

"He's got plenty of bad with him today," Nain said as we ran, reaffirming what I was already feeling. "Like I said: take everything you can. Time to become as scary as I always knew you could be."

I nodded, and we ran into the factory, and found ourselves in the middle of a war zone.

CHAPTER SIXTEEN

The first super we ran past had the ability to cut her enemies using nothing more than her mind, I realized after a large gash appeared on my thigh out of nowhere.

Handy.

I turned to her and smiled. I forced my way into her mind. Found what I was looking for, took what I wanted.

So easy. Candy from a baby. I felt her power singing alongside my own, the fire I'd taken from the pyro. Strengthened, fed.

"Next," I said, running toward where I saw Brennan, Ada, and Stone fighting, back to back, in the middle of the chaos.

My main focus was on reaching Ada, Brennan, and Stone. I saw Nain barrel in a different direction, easily figured out who his focus was.

A demon stood off to the side, flanked by other demons, a few other beings. He was not exceptionally tall. He wore his demonic form: dark grayish-blue skin. Two small horns at the top of his head. Eyes that glowed a malevolent red as they settled on his old enemy.

I heard Ada grunt, and tore my attention away from the two demons. I ran toward my friends. Ada was pushing herself to the limit, doing her best to hold a shield that would protect herself and Stone and Brennan from the barrage of attacks being leveled at them. She was doing an amazing job, but a shield that strong takes a crazy amount of power. She wouldn't be able to hold it much longer under that level of stress.

Time to remove some of the stress, I thought to myself. I easily cut down a couple of lower demons who kept hitting at the shield with crude axes. There was a pyro here. I already had one, but why not add another to my collection. I entered her mind, stole her powers, and left an empty husk behind.

Well, that got their attention.

Most of the assholes attacking my friends turned and came toward me. Some were nothing more than human thugs, attracted by Astaroth's slick words and promises. Those, I knocked out easily by going into their heads and shutting them down.

That left a few more demons, a guy who had just displayed a power I badly wanted (the ability to leap far and fast when he needed to) and a chick who was throwing chunks of concrete around with nothing but her mind. I'd take that, too.

The demons charged me, and I fought them off with a combination of fists and fire. I glanced to the side, and happened to see Bashiok and Dahael destroying a demon with tiny knives I'd never even known they had. They both seemed to be enjoying themselves.

As I tossed fire at the final demon in front of me, I also ripped the power from the telekinetic. I was feeling it now, all of this power singing in me, coursing through me along with my connection to Nain.

I felt invincible.

I ripped powers from a few more supers (Astaroth seemed to have a thing for those with some kind of fire power. I took it all.) and then practiced with them, destroying the demons that were still bashing at Ada's shield. It did not take long, and the relief I felt from Ada was palpable.

I looked around. A crowd had gathered around Astaroth and Nain, who were going at it with fists. Both bloody, both angry.

I glanced at Brennan, Ada, and Stone, nodded to the group around the two demons. We could remove that threat while Nain had his playtime with Astaroth. They nodded, and we ran, together, into yet another group of nutjobs who wanted to kill us.

Just another day at the office.

As we got closer, I could hear Nain and Astaroth snarling at each other, taunting each other. They were both in pain. I considered ending it right then.

Not yet, Molls. Give me more time, Nain said in my mind. I was both irritated and pleased that he knew me so well. I watched as he pummeled Astaroth. He seemed to be enjoying it. His rage flooded me, fed me.

Astaroth backed away from Nain, and his eyes landed on me. He smiled. "What are you going to do, little demoness? This is not a fight you can win."

Nain punched him in the face, hard, and that was the end of Astaroth's taunts for me. I destroyed a few more of his demons in response. I surveyed his remaining crew: demons, a few more supers with powers I could take. And witches, who he must have been keeping in reserve for something exactly like this. Shit.

Astaroth laughed. "Just die quietly, demon bitch."

"I don't do that type of thing. Only one of us is dying today," I said, making sure that I kept Nain in sight. This was coming to an end, very soon.

I felt confusion from Astaroth. "Doesn't she know–"

And Nain punched him in the face again, ending whatever he was going to say. At that moment, I felt something beautiful from Astaroth: fear.

I lost track of how long we fought. I threw fire only to have it turned to flame moths by the witches. Stone bashed into the witches, but never quickly enough to save my fire. Nain rampaged against Astaroth, fighting his old friend and worst enemy in a dizzying barrage of hits, kicks, avoiding Astaroth's attacks as best he could. But he was cut, and weakening. Brennan ran through the crowd of witches and warlocks, gnawing out throats, snapping at tendons. He bled. Ada tried to shield us from the attacks, both magical and physical, coming at us while trying to keep herself alive.

The crew was weakening.

I was the only one gaining strength, just as Nain had planned it. The pain around me, the fear, the amount of power I had consumed filled me. I gritted my teeth against it. I felt like I was about to split. And I knew that Nain knew it, too.

I can't hold anymore. I'm about to lose it, I thought desperately at him.

He looked across the factory at me, our eyes meeting for just a moment through the chaos of battle.

I felt determination, anger from him. Resignation. *It's time.*

I turned toward Astaroth. Watched him swing an axe toward Nain. Nain just smiled at him, a feral, terrifying smile. Victorious.

He winked at me, then he looked at Astaroth again. "Check mate, motherfucker."

Now, Molly.

And I raged. I unleashed everything I had on him. Fire, energy, mental knives, fear. I threw it all at Astaroth and heard him scream.

And then I felt Nain's anguish flood through me. Pain, terror, loss.

I love you Molly. I'm sorry.

Agony. Burning, searing, ripping pain.

And then I felt him drift away.

I halted my attack on Astaroth, ran to where I'd last seen Nain, just moments before.

All that was left of him, and of Astaroth a few feet away, was ash, still smoldering.

Nothing.

Gone.

I stared at it for a few panicked seconds in disbelief. I bit down hard on my lip, trying to control myself, hold it together. I failed. I screamed into the emptiness of the factory, my anguish reverberating off of the walls, steel girders above. The building shook around me, chunks of concrete falling from the deteriorated ceiling. I felt part of my soul hemorrhaging — such a physical thing I swore I'd be able to see it if I could just open my eyes.

Emptiness.

My scream lasted for what felt like an eternity, ending only when I'd shredded my vocal chords beyond use. I buried my hands in the pile of ash that had been the man I loved, squeezed it in my hands as if wishing hard enough would bring him back to me. As if I could feel close to him one last time.

Nothing.

When I opened my eyes, I saw the team staring at me, at what was left of Nain, in horror and sadness. Their ears were bleeding.

"Honey," Ada said, tears streaming down her face. "I saw it, Molly. You didn't do it. When you hit Astaroth, whatever was happening to him happened to Nain. You didn't do that. Astaroth did," she said desperately. "You didn't do it." She started crying, gasping.

"I saw it too," Stone said through a voice choked with emotion. "Oh, Christ." And then he broke down. Brennan, still in wolf form, howled mournfully into the emptiness.

The Guardians soared into the building, freed Nain and Astaroth from the mortal realm. Eunomia stayed after her sisters left, watching me.

I felt my rage growing. Pure rage, something wild, fatal in its intent. Astaroth's minions were running out of the warehouse.

They did not make it out alive.

It only took an instant. No effort at all. Instinct. Bodies burned around me.

"Molly!" Ada called. I turned to her, caught a reflection of myself in the remains of a broken window behind her. My eyes glowed white. A snarl on my lips, and fire flowing over my body, part of me and ready to do my bidding. I turned away.

"Molly, no!"

I looked down at my hands. The hematite ring he'd placed on my finger, the one that signified our unending devotion to each other, was cool against my skin. His ashes stained my palms.

My heart was gone.

Vengeance would be mine. I walked out into the night, my imps and Eunomia following me.

I turned to her. "You will not interfere."

She shook her head. "I will not. The Nether will be a busy place this night."

I nodded, stalked out into the night powered by nothing but rage and loss. It was all I had left.

EPILOGUE

"We're receiving reports of a massive fire in the Morningside neighborhood of Detroit, where investigators say they've uncovered several bodies of what look at this point to be wild animals..." (Fox 2 News, Detroit)

"Molly. You should eat something, baby girl."

"I can't even describe the scene here in East English Village. This house, which neighbors claim was a quiet place, now something out of a nightmare. Police this morning found the bodies of several women, at least a dozen according to latest reports, of various ages. An unidentified Detroit Police Department official tells us that there were several satanic ritual items in the home, and police are considering this the scene of a mass suicide, possibly a cult ceremony...." (Channel 7 Action News, Detroit)

"Mistress must feed. Wifey and I find demon for you. Gotta get strong."

"It's really impossible to say what happened here last night. There are fifty-three men in the apartment building behind me. All dead, and, from what investigators are telling us, there is no visible sign of death. One theory is that a gas leak is to blame...." (Channel 4 News, Detroit)

"Molly. Come on kid. You're needed. He wouldn't have wanted this for you."

"I'm telling you: there's something freaky going on around here. Those fires? Heard some guy saying he swore he saw The Angel leaving the area, she hasn't been seen since. Where's she been?" (Caller, WDET's "The Craig Fahle Show")

"Molly, we were thinking of having a memorial service. There are so many who want to pay their respects...is that okay? Father Balester thinks it might be good for you."

"You know what I think? There's more out there than we realize. I think all sorts of beings walk among us, and maybe we're just getting our first glimpse of what they can do."

"All right. Thank you. Very interesting viewpoints from downtown Detroit. Back to Bob and Kelly in the studio."

"Well, Bob? What do you say? Are we surrounded by supernaturals?"

"Sure. Just today, I saw a witch on Woodward! *laughter*" (WWJ Radio, Detroit)

"I remember when they stopped fighting, all of a sudden, you know? Nain asked me if I could lift the enchantment from him, but I wasn't able to. I didn't know what it did. All I knew was that it seemed to end their constant battles. I wasn't strong enough. I should have tried harder, done more. Damn him."

"Police chief Jones says today that he will be looking into the possibility of supernatural activity in the city of Detroit."

"Something's not right here. I'm going to find out what it is. I swear it to the people of this city. I will find out." (Fox 2 News, Detroit)

"I know you want to follow him. We need you, Molly. We can't lose you too."

Dear Molly,

If you're reading this, then that means that I'm not with you anymore. I want to destroy, just thinking about this, knowing it's coming and that I'm going to hurt you in the worst way possible.

I warned you that you would hate me for the things I'd ask you to do. I am fine with you hating me. You're alive, and that's all that has ever mattered to me. I tried to think of a way out of this. There is none. Astaroth does not give up. I've seen him when he has a grudge. You never would have been safe. That is not acceptable to me. He had to die so you could live, and, as you've now undoubtedly figured out, if he dies, so do I. Fucking demon and his fucking enchantments.

I hate this.

We never had a chance to do so many things. Time wasn't on our side. Why couldn't I have found you a few hundred years ago?

I love you. I am shit at showing it sometimes. I wish I'd spent more time being the man you deserved.

So many times, I told myself to stay away from you. Once it was clear that it was Astaroth we were dealing with, I knew this was the way it would have to end. And I knew it would destroy you when it did. I wasn't strong

211

enough to stay away from you, to leave you alone so this would hurt you less when it happened.

I've never wanted anything, anyone, as much as I want you. I never knew that I could need someone the way I need you. It would have been so much better for you if I had kept my distance.

I always have been a selfish bastard.

Do not blame yourself. I know you. You're blaming yourself for this, and you're the only one who doesn't deserve any blame. Blame Astaroth. Blame me for making you do something I never would have been strong enough to live with if the situations were reversed. Blame the witch who put the enchantment on us. Blame any of us. Not you.

You are amazing. You are sunlight streaming through the clouds, warmth on the coldest night. There is nothing like being wrapped in your arms, or those moments when your eyes meet mine and I forget to breathe because I'm lost. The curve of your lower lip when you smile, the contented way you sigh when I kiss you. It doesn't even matter that demons have no chance at "heaven" or whatever the afterlife is called. I've already had mine, because of you.

I love you so much, Molly.

Always,
Bael

"It is not your time yet, demon girl. I am sorry."

"Be with me always – take any form – drive me mad!
only do not leave me in this abyss, where I cannot find
you! Oh, God! it is unutterable! I can not live without my
life! I can not live without my soul!"

Emily Bronte
Wuthering Heights

END OF BOOK ONE

Continue reading for a sneak peek at Book Two in the Hidden series:

BROKEN

BROKEN: CHAPTER ONE

My name is Molly Brooks.
Vigilante.
Demon.
Mindflayer.

I killed the man I love. Ended the lives of every enemy he'd had, in one fiery, bloody night.

It did not bring him back to me.

My friends, the team of supernaturals who followed the demon they knew as the Nain Rouge, tiptoe around me. They want me to eat. They want me to tell them what to do, where to go, the way my love used to. They want me to feed.
I will never feed from another.

I will keep this city safe, in his honor.

I will die trying.

I can only hope that it happens sooner, rather than later.
My wrath is absolute, my lust for death, pain, fear,

unending.

I have lost myself.

I have been lied to, used, left behind, by the being I loved most in this world.

And this thing I have become...this is exactly what Nain always knew I would be.

Damn him for making me do this without him.

Six months, exactly, since the day I lost Nain. The day I destroyed him. The day I realized how far he would go to get what he wanted. I'd be lying if I said I didn't hate him. I'd also be lying if I said I didn't love him, didn't miss him so much it hurt.

I'd spent the first two months like a zombie. I stayed in his room, surrounded by his scent. I didn't speak. I didn't eat. I didn't feed.

And, yet, here I am.

Death would not come for me, the way I hoped it would. So I did the one thing that would make me feel better: I hunted. My imps found demons, warlocks, vampires for me, and I destroyed them. Each kill momentarily made me feel better.

But they didn't ease the pain I felt when I laid in bed at night, alone.

The gaping wound in my soul, the one left when our marriage bond had been severed at his death...well. It never stops hurting. It is eternal pain. This is the cost of the marriage bond between demons.

I am living a half-life.

That night, I fed, took powers by force. I truly became

a mindflayer, a nightmare among nightmares. Power flows through my body, and I can kill in dozens of ways with little more than a thought. But it wasn't just my mind, my powers, that changed under the stress of losing Nain.

I changed.

I am afraid of myself. I will not use my powers anymore. The temptation to do more of what I did that night is overwhelming.

But I still hunt. I go back to the way I used to do things: blades and fists. The only difference now is that I have no qualms about killing my prey. I destroy those who would cause harm to the people of his city.

Tonight, six months after Nain's death, I hunt werewolves. I revel in their pain and fear, and their deaths fill me, for a time. Their blood stains the ground around me, bodies litter the street. The Guardians arrive and claim their souls, even before I've left the scene.

And then I go home, and I am alone, hungry, and afraid again.

Sleep is not the friend it once was.

It won't come easily. And when it does, I am not granted the deep, dreamless sleep of the peaceful.

There are the nightmares. Nain dying, over and over again in slow motion as I realize what I've done. Brennan rips my limbs from my body. My friends stare, mutter "murderer" over and over again.

But I'll take these nightmares over the sweet dreams.

The dreams in which I am wrapped in his arms, my legs tangled with his, and it feels so real I swear I can smell him. And then I wake up. For just a moment, I am happy. And then reality sets in, and I've lost him all over again.

I finished hunting werewolves, and retreated to the roof of the loft. Ready to spend quality time with my punching bag. Another thing that always made me feel better.

I don't know how many hours I spent whaling away at the punching bag Stone installed for me after Nain's death. When I wasn't beating up on bad guys, this was my place.

My knuckles bled, healed, cracked, and bled again. My arms were tired, but not tired enough to make me stop. Constant motion, hitting, was the only thing keeping me sane. I stopped punching, looked up at the sky. It was probably a little after three A.M. I'd been at it since I got home from taking out the werewolves a little after midnight.

I punched the bag again. Harder. I would not cry.

Before Nain, I'd been so good at avoiding feeling things. I had managed to keep emotions, mine and others, in their own compartment. I recognized them, but they didn't affect me.

He changed everything.

I stopped punching for a minute, rested my forehead against the punching bag. The air around me was frigid. It didn't matter. My breath formed clouds in the dark night.

I tried to remember to breathe. I wished I could stop. Stop breathing, stop feeling, stop living. Just, stop.

I felt Brennan's presence nearby. Shook my head, tried to pull myself together, and started punching again. Sure enough, within seconds, the roof door was opening, and he strolled out, dressed, as usual, in jeans and a flannel shirt. I glanced at him, continued whaling on the bag.

"Are you going to sleep at some point tonight, or spend all night up here, hitting things?" he asked, leaning against the wall.

"Am I keeping you up, Bren?" I asked, well aware of the snarl in my voice.

He shook his head, watched me for a while in silence. I kept punching, hoping he'd go away.

"You've been up here every night for weeks. You're busy the rest of the time with meetings and keeping this place running and fighting big bads. Everyone has to sleep sometimes."

"I sleep when I need to." This, along with everything else in my life, had changed with Nain's death and its aftermath. Meeting Nain had helped me tap into my powers, and losing and avenging him had taken them a step further. Or, a few hundred steps further.

I barely felt human at all any more.

"You're going to eventually lose your temper and incinerate that one," he said, gesturing at the bag I was hitting. "And then Stone will put another one up for you, and he'll be happy because it gives him something to do for a while and he can feel useful again."

"He's busy enough. He's still out there kicking ass."

"But you're keeping him away from the really bad stuff. That's the stuff he lives for, and you know that. You take all the bad shit, and you leave him and the rest of us with the supernatural equivalent of traffic stops."

I stopped punching and looked at him, finally. "I'm not in any hurry to lose anyone else right now. I'm sorry if that offends you, Brennan. And if you're here to lecture me again, you need to leave. Because I'll be honest," I said, hitting the bag so hard it swung, creaking on its chains. "I'm really not in the mood tonight."

"Six months," he said quietly. "You're not the only one who's been keeping track." We stood in silence for a few minutes. "Sometimes it feels like we lost both of you that night. Those first weeks afterward, you were a zombie. Now, you're like a machine. We all understand. We're mourning him, too."

"Did you strike the blow that killed him?"

Brennan just looked at me.

"Then you have no goddamned idea how I feel."

"You know as well as I do that he knew it would happen that way," he said quietly. I sensed nervousness in him. "He knew it would kill him, and he told you to do it anyway."

I turned away. "How did you know that?"

"He left me a letter. Father Balester delivered it, after. He knew."

"I know he did. I got to hear his thoughts as he died."

"So maybe you should stop blaming yourself. Maybe you should blame him for putting you into that situation. Or maybe you should blame whoever was ordering Astaroth to capture you. But you can't keep blaming yourself for something you had no control over." He paused. "And that last part is something I do have experience with, and you know I do."

Of course I did. I still had the nightmares when I did manage to doze off to prove it. "And have you stopped feeling guilty yet?"

"No."

"And you didn't even manage to kill me," I said, meeting his eyes, then turning back to the punching bag.

READ MORE IN
HIDDEN BOOK TWO
BROKEN

Visit http://www.colleenvanderlinden.com/hidden for news, updates, and more

Never Miss an Update!

Sign up for the Hidden Newsletter.
http://bit.ly/hiddennewsletter

For backstory material, news, and upcoming events be sure to check out http://www.colleenvanderlinden.com/hidden.

ABOUT THE AUTHOR

Colleen Vanderlinden is the author and publisher of the *Hidden* series, which currently includes *Lost Girl, Broken, Home, Forever Night, and Strife*. She lives in the Detroit area with her husband, children, and two lazy cats. She enjoys reading, obsessing over comic book characters, gardening, and playing World of Warcraft.

Website: http://www.colleenvanderlinden.com
Facebook: facebook.com/colleenvanderlinden
Twitter: @C_Vanderlinden

The Hidden Series

Book One: Lost Girl
Book Two: Broken
Book Three: Home
Book 3.5: Forever Night
Book Four: Strife
Book Five: Nether - Available Fall 2014

Made in the USA
San Bernardino, CA
25 June 2014